Viral Revelations: Ra-E's Visions Omnibus Trilogy

Viral Revelations: Ra-E's Visions, Volume 4

Maxwell Hoffman

Published by Maxwell Hoffman, 2024.

This is a work of fiction. Similarities to real people, places, or events are entirely coincidental.

VIRAL REVELATIONS: RA-E'S VISIONS OMNIBUS TRILOGY

First edition. November 14, 2024.

Copyright © 2024 Maxwell Hoffman.

ISBN: 979-8230135166

Written by Maxwell Hoffman.

Also by Maxwell Hoffman

Acorn Man Savior of the Forest
Acorn Man Savior of the Forest

Amir Laurent: Fowl Play a Cuckoo Tale
Amir Laurent: Fowl Play A Cuckoo Tale Book 1 Opal's Deception

Arctic Shadows: A Lenin Aslanov Story
Arctic Shadows: A Lenin Aslanov Story Book 1: The Finnish Incursion
Arctic Shadows: A Lenin Aslanov Story Book 2 Dmitry's Temper
Arctic Shadows: A Lenin Aslanov Story Book 3 Journey to Iceland

Baron Floofnose: A Capybara's Quest
Baron Floofnose: A Capybara's Quest Omnibus Trilogy

Bellamy's Blunders: Adjusting to Society
Bellamy's Blunders: Adjusting to Society Omnibus Trilogy

Benny Dubious Playbook Scheme Series 3
Benny Dubious Playbook Scheme Trouble in Georgia Book 2: "Moshie's" Fall
Benny Dubious Playbook Scheme Trouble in Georgia Book 3: Hugo's Revelation

Benny Dubiuos Playbook Scheme Nevada Shuffle
Benny Dubious Playbook Scheme: Nevada Shuffle

Frozen Dawn: A Neanderthal's Redemption
Frozen Dawn: A Neanderthal's Redemption Omnibus Trilogy

Ivan Zhuk: Zhuk's Gambit
Ivan Zhuk: Zhuk's Gambit Book 1 Mental Agony
Ivan Zhuk: Zhuk's Gambit Book 2 The MMA Fighter
Ivan Zhuk: Zhuk's Gambit Book 3 Ivan's Freedom

Knox Sovereign: The Juche Wars
Knox Sovereign: The Juche Wars Book 1 Unmasking Knox Sovereign
Knox Sovereign: The Juche Wars Book 2 A Daring Rescue
Knox Sovereign: The Juche Wars Book 3: Fall of Colonel Rex MacManners

Misadventures of Wolfgang Wirrarr
Misadventures of Wolfgang Wirrarr Omnibus Trilogy

Rowan Sunfire Frosty Fugitive Series
Rowan Sunfire Frosty Fugitive Book 3 Defense of Vos Tower
Rowan Sunfire Frosty Fugitive Omnibus Trilogy

Viral Revelations: Ra-E's Visions
Viral Revelations: Ra-E's Visions Omnibus Trilogy

Wiccan Guardian
Wiccan Guardian Omnibus Trilogy

Watch for more at https://www.instagram.com/vader7800/.

Table of Contents

Viral Revelations: Ra-E's Visions Omnibus Trilogy 1
Part One 4
Prologue 5
Chapter One 13
Chapter Two 21
Chapter Three 30
Part Two 39
Chapter Four 40
Chapter Five 49
Chapter Six 58
Chapter Seven 67
Part Three 75
Chapter Eight 76
Chapter Nine 84
Chapter Ten 92
Epilogue 101
Part One 109
Prologue 110
Chapter One 118
Chapter Two 125
Chapter Three 133
Part Two 140
Chapter Five 150
Chapter Six 160
Chapter Seven 168
Part Three 177
Chapter Eight 178
Chapter Nine 187
Chapter Ten 195
Epilogue 203
Part One 210
Prologue 211
Chapter One 220

Chapter Two 228
Chapter Three 238
Part Two 246
Chapter Four 247
Chapter Five 257
Chapter Six 267
Chapter Seven 275
Part Three 282
Chapter Eight 283
Chapter Nine 292
Chapter Ten 301
Epilogue 309

VIRAL REVELATIONS: RA-E'S VISIONS
OMNIBUS TRILOGY
BY
Maxwell Hoffman

VIRAL REVELATIONS: RA-E'S VISIONS GAME 1
SANTIAGO AWARE
by
Maxwell Hoffman

Part One

Prologue

Unbelievable!

Santiago Ramirez was taken back by the presence of Ra-E, the AI virus that was observing his actions in the previous series. He couldn't believe that such a virus existed or had major concerns for him.

"SO YOU'RE TELLING ME my entire world is made up?!" cried Santiago.

RA-E NODS WITH SADNESS.

"YOU MUST BE SO SAD to hear that" said Ra-E.

ON THE CONTRARY, SANTIAGO was pleased to hear that. It was no wonder why Baron Floofnose got the upper hand every single time! The anthropomorphic capybara was always so crafty and smart!

"IT ALL MAKES SENSE!" chuckled Santiago.

SANTIAGO COULD UNDERSTAND why the commune workers left him and even why the Venezuelan soldiers stopped assisting him! His farm was crumbling to the point where it was going to be beyond repair. But the farmer knew he had to do something, anything to change the situation. He darted towards the front door of his farm to see a notice on it.

"NOTICE: THIS PROPERTY will soon belong to the State Government of Venezuela. Have a Nice Day!"

SANTIAGO COULDN'T BELIEVE the government was foreclosing on his farm! He had to do something against Baron Floofnose and fast!

Ra-E's Plan

THE AI VIRUS WANTED his new friend - Santiago Ramirez to relax for a moment.

"ENOUGH OF THIS PANIC" said Ra-E as he slapped Santiago in the face.

"THANKS, I NEEDED THAT" said Santiago, "but what are we going to do about this foreclosure? I can't do anything against Baron Floofnose with this!"

"LUCKY FOR YOU I ALREADY induced the capybara into a night terror trance" continued Ra-E, "giving him a night terror would preoccupy him for the moment while you handle all of this."

"OH THANK YOU" SAID Santiago.

SANTIAGO DECIDED TO head towards a computer to check his assets. As the farmer gazed at it, he noticed his bank account was locked.

"I CAN'T ACCESS MY BANK!" cried Santiago.

RA-E SIGHED AND WITH a snap of a finger, he was able to access it.

"PAY A FEW BILLS HERE and there first before we do anything against the pesky capybara" continued Ra-E.

"YOU GOT IT BOSS" CONTINUED Santiago.

AS SANTIAGO CONTINUED to pay a few bills he owed, he would hope it would get the proper notice from the government not to foreclose on the farm. Meanwhile in a secret location in Caracas, the nameless government official gazed at his monitor and noticed Santiago was paying off what he owed.

A Change of Heart

THE NAMELESS GOVERNMENT official knew he couldn't fully allow Santiago to operate but allow him to operate enough so that he could live.

"ALL I CAN DO IS JUST extend the foreclosure to another 90 days" continued the nameless government official.

IT WAS THE SAME NAMELESS government official who had observed Santiago's failed actions against Den Town in the jungle not far from the capital. The same mystery figures didn't seem to enjoy seeing the failure over all of this. But they were surprised he was paying bills on time.

"I SUPPOSE WE SHOULD allow him to continue to operate under a limited supply" added the first mystery figure.

"OH, I AGREE" SAID THE second mystery figure.

"YES, YES GO FORWARD with it" said the third mystery figure.

THE THREE MYSTERY FIGURES agreed for a temporary truce unaware that Ra-E was the one who allowed the actions to continue. The Venezuelan government or this version of the government didn't realize they were all fakes! But it didn't matter to the likes of Santiago Ramirez who was thrilled to see his status was reactivated! The farmer was thrilled as he sat back watching them reactivate his account!

Thanking the AI

SANTIAGO WAS THRILLED, he was with joy as he began to dance around his farmhouse. Ra-E thought it was odd but he went with it.

"I'M CURIOUS TO KNOW why you are so happy?" asked Ra-E.

"THANKS TO YOU MY BILLS are paid and soon we can see what Baron Floofnose is up to!" chuckled Santiago.

"OH YEA, GOOD THING I have that ability in this world" chuckled Ra-E.

"SAY YOU WERE CREATED by a hacker, who's the hacker's name?" asked Santiago.

"HIS NAME IS TAMAR AL-Barqawi, much like you he in the real world has an issue with his employer" continued Ra-E, "so he decided to get back at them by creating me to infect this game to help you!"

"WELL, I DON'T SEE IT as a problem!" chuckled Santiago, "I do see it as a problem for Baron Floofnose!"

"OH MOST CERTAINLY, I intend to become the problem for him and those who have wronged you in the past" chuckled Ra-E.

"YES, WE BOTH AGREE on something" chuckled Santiago, "now let's get down to business and actually go after that pesky capybara!"

"WE NEED TO FOCUS ON the one person who could assist him a pesky vet known as Marianna Torres!" continued Ra-E.

Chapter One

Enter Dr. Stuffynose

Meanwhile back in Den Town, which was just a few paces away from Santiago Ramirez's own farm, Baron Floofnose the once proud hero of Den Town was suffering from a series of night terrors. The night terrors were given to him by Ra-E as a ruse to incapacitate the anthropomorphic capybara. Dr. Stuffynose, a local capybara doctor soon entered the residence of the Floofnoses.

"OH, THANK GOODNESS you have arrived doctor" said Julie as she greeted him.

"YES" SAID DR. STUFFYNOSE, "where is the patient?"

"UPSTAIRS" CONTINUED Julie.

JULIE ESCORTED THE doctor to the second floor, her children - Kerri and Vice were eager to observe from their rooms. But they had to slam their doors shut once Julie escorted the doctor towards the main bedroom. There Baron sat in bed, he couldn't believe he was reduced to this!

"I AM GLAD YOU CALLED me" said Dr. Stuffynose.

DR. STUFFYNOSE THEN began to take out his usual doctor equipment from his bag and began to examine Baron. Even giving him a blood pressure test.

"WELL, IT SEEMS LIKE your vital signs are normal" continued Dr. Stuffynose.

"I DON'T UNDERSTAND what's causing these night terrors to happen" continued Baron.

The Night Terrors

BARON CONTINUES TO explain to Dr. Stuffynose that he always ends up in the jungle during his dreams. Surrounded by an unseen force that has been observing his actions since the first series.

"WHAT SORT OF UNSEEN force are you speaking of?" asked Dr. Stuffynose who was rather skeptical of everything.

"I HAVE NO IDEA" ADDED Baron, "but ever since I managed to defeat Santiago Ramirez, these strange night terrors have been happening."

"OH IT'S HORRIBLE DOCTOR, he woke up in the middle of the night for the past few evenings" continued Julie.

THERE WAS NOTHING THAT Dr. Stuffynose could do with his own expertise. However, the doctor knew from the Mayor of a vet in Caracas that could assist him. Ms. Marianna Torres!

"THERE IS ONE HUMAN we can all trust" said Dr. Stuffynose, "Ms. Marianna Torres, she could be the key on unlocking what's causing your night terrors. In the mean time, I suggest you drink some tea and try to get some rest."

"BUT WHAT IF THE NIGHT terrors happen again?" asked Baron.

"JUST TRY TO THINK CALM thoughts" continued Dr. Stuffynose.

THE CAPYBARA DOCTOR soon heads out of the room.

Julie's Suspicions

JULIE FLOOFNOSE HAD some ideas on who was responsible for all of these night terrors - Santiago Ramirez or at least an unseen force helping him! She couldn't believe the farmer would stoop this low since his defeat.

"I HAVE A FEW IDEAS on who might be helping causing these night terrors" said Julie.

"OH, WHO DO YOU HAVE in mind?" asked Dr. Stuffynose.

"THE FARMER" CONTINUED Julie.

DR. STUFFYNOSE WAS puzzled, sure Santiago Ramirez was a terrible farmer willing to do whatever it takes for the Venezuelan government to get rid of Den Town. But would he stoop so low to use magic of some sort to drive Baron Floofnose mad?

"I AM SKEPTICAL OF ALL of this" added Dr. Stuffynose, "your husband must be facing some sort of trauma issues with the farmer."

"BUT I FEEL IT IN MY gut that some unseen force is helping the farmer" continued Julie.

THE CAPYBARA DOCTOR continued to dismiss Julie's suspicions.

"I WILL GO TO CARACAS and seek out the vet" continued Dr. Stuffynose, "you keep your husband safe."

THE CHILDREN OF THE Floofnose residence also knew some sort of strange unseen force was assisting Santiago Ramirez.

Capybara Children Debate

NEITHER KERRI NOR VICE didn't know what else to do as they paced back and forth in their rooms. Once Julie led Dr. Stuffynose downstairs they finally were able to get out of their rooms to speak to each other.

"THE DOCTOR DOESN'T see it, but we do" said Kerri.

"YEA, POPS IS BEING induced in a strange magical spell" chuckled Vice.

"MAGIC, I DON'T KNOW if it is magic" continued Kerri, "but it is still disturbing nonetheless."

"HOW ABOUT WE SNEAK off in the middle of the night to investigate the farmer?" asked Vice.

KERRI THOUGHT FOR A moment, they could get in so much trouble with their parents. But they were desperate to help their father out.

"OKAY, YOU GOT IT" SAID Kerri, "we'll sneak out in the evening."

THE TWO FLOOFNOSE CHILDREN agreed to disobey their parents in order to save one of them. As night fell, the two Floofnose children managed to sneak out of the house. The capybara police officers were on patrol looking out for anything suspicious. The two Floofnose children had to duck around buildings as a way of not being spotted.

Chapter Two

Into the Jungle

Both Floofnose children arrived and headed into the jungle to get to the farmhouse just beyond it. They could see the debris from the last fight that their father Baron Floofnose had with the Venezuelan military and commune workers. It was now a thing of the past to them.

"WE HAVE TO HURRY, THIS way through all of the brush" said Kerri.

VICE FOLLOWED HIS SISTER, they darted around the brush and finally made it through the jungle. It was quiet, a bit too quiet around the farmhouse. They sensed some unease as they began to creep towards the house.

"SOMETHING DOESN'T FEEL right" said Vice.

VICE WAS FRIGHTEN BY the sudden silence, he knew this was a bad sign. But Kerri wanted to expose what was helping Santiago Ramirez do this to their father.

"YOU'RE NOT CHICKEN are you?" asked Kerri to Vice.

"NO" REPLIED VICE.

"THEN LET'S CONTINUE" said Kerri.

AS THE FLOOFNOSE CHILDREN darted around to a window, they gazed inside. There the notorious farmer was there - Santiago Ramirez! Santiago had a happy grin on his face. Neither of them liked that grin at all, he then turned to a strange figure in the other room.

The Strange Figure

NEITHER OF THE TWO Floofnose children could identify who was the strange figure in the other room. But they had some idea that this was the unseen force assisting Santiago Ramirez causing the night terrors for their father! They wanted to listen into the conversation Santiago was having.

"I AM SO HAPPY YOU WERE able to prevent the government from foreclosing on my farm!" chuckled Santiago.

"YES" SAID RA-E, "IT'S a good thing I did intervene on terms of changing the entire system in your favor."

"SO WHAT'S NEXT ON OUR agenda now that my bills are all out of the way?" asked Santiago.

"WE STRIKE AT BARON Floofnose at his weakest!" continued Ra-E, "I have already induced the capybara with night terrors making him inoperable."

"BUT HOW WILL I GO INTO Den Town?" asked Santiago.

"OH YOU WILL, IN BARON'S own dreams!" chuckled Ra-E, "With my powers, you can travel there and cause as much mischief and misery as much as you please!"

"OH GOODIE!" CHUCKLED Santiago.

SANTIAGO WAS THRILLED with the AI virus at his side. The capybara children were terrified by this development! How did this being come about they both thought!

Warning Mother

BOTH FLOOFNOSE CHILDREN knew they had to head back to Den Town not being seen at all. As they darted around the farm, they eventually made their way back into the jungle.

"WE HAVE TO TELL MOTHER!" cried Vice.

"YES, I THINK SHE ALREADY suspects this!" added Kerri.

BOTH CAPYBARA CHILDREN were unaware that Ra-E knew they were there. It was because the AI virus wanted them to fear his presence! Santiago didn't know the capybara children were there but the AI virus knew otherwise.

"I THINK WE MIGHT HAVE been spied upon by some unwanted pests" said Ra-E as he gazed around.

"IMPOSSIBLE" SAID SANTIAGO.

SANTIAGO FELT DEN TOWN needed to be taught a lesson, why not through his new friend Ra-E? Meanwhile for the Floofnose children, they arrived home with Julie noticing them through the kitchen.

"YOU TWO, DID YOU TWO sneak out of your rooms?" asked Julie.

"WE HAD TO" SAID KERRI.

"YEA, WE'RE WORRIED for papa!" added Vice.

JULIE FELT SADDEN FOR her children.

"I KNOW YOU TWO WERE trying to do the right thing" said Julie, "but it's dangerous out there especially with that farmer still around."

"WE'RE SORRY" SAID BOTH of the Floofnose children.

Baron's Latest Night Terror

MEANWHILE UPSTAIRS, Baron was having another traumatic night terror!

"GET AWAY FROM ME!" cried Baron.

BARON USED HIS MIGHTY teeth to chew through his pillow by mistake. The commotion brought Julie, Kerri and Vice to witnesses the strange behavior.

"OH DEAR!" CRIED JULIE.

THE FLOOFNOSE CHILDREN were in shock and frighten for their father's safety.

⟨ ⟩

"DON'T WORRY FATHER, whoever is doing this to you we will make them pay" said Kerri.

⟨ ⟩

"I AM UNSURE YOU CAN'T do a thing against whatever is causing these night terrors to happen to me" continued Baron, "worse whatever is behind it can do the same to you!"

⟨ ⟩

THE FLOOFNOSE CHILDREN were taken back by these comments. Baron had a point, the same fate could await them if they were not careful. Meanwhile in Caracas, Dr. Stuffynose had managed to look up the apartment of Dr. Marianna Torres. He rang the doorbell and soon she answered.

⟨ ⟩

"EXCUSE ME, CAN I HELP you?" asked Marianna.

⟨ ⟩

"FELLOW DOCTOR, I AM Dr. Stuffynose of Den Town, I need your assistance" continued Dr. Stuffynose.

⟨ ⟩

"WITH WHAT?" ASKED MARIANNA.

⟨ ⟩

"APPARENTLY MY CLIENT Baron Floofnose is facing a series of night terrors and could use your assistance" continued Dr. Stuffynose.

⟨ ⟩

"YES, I WILL HELP YOU" said Marianna as she remembered the capybaras, "just let me pack my things."

Chapter Three

Traveling to Den Town

⟨ ⟩

Ms. Marianna Torres knew she had to follow the strange anthropomorphic capybara doctor known as Dr. Stuffynose. She thought it was rather odd and humorous that Den Town would have its own cute rodent doctor.

⟨ ⟩

"THIS WAY MS. TORRES" said Dr. Stuffynose.

⟨ ⟩

BOTH DOCTORS SOON PASSED the farmer's farmhouse, they could see something was strange going on inside.

⟨ ⟩

"DO YOU THINK WE SHOULD investigate?" asked Marianna.

⟨ ⟩

"NOT OF OUR CONCERN at the moment" continued Dr. Stuffynose.

⟨ ⟩

THE CAPYBARA DOCTOR then led Marianna through the jungle. It was still dark on where they were stepping and they had to be careful with every step within the darkness. Marianna sensed she was being watched but she couldn't tell who.

⟨ ⟩

"EVERYTHING ALRIGHT?" asked Dr. Stuffynose.

⟨ ⟩

"I'M FINE, BUT I THINK someone might be watching us" added Marianna.

⟨ ⟩

DR. STUFFYNOSE CHUCKLED at the notion.

⟨ ⟩

"THERE IS NO SUCH THINGS as ghost" said Dr. Stuffynose.

⟨ ⟩

MARIANNA SHRUGGED IT off, but in reality it was Ra-E who was observing them through a small portal on the chalkboard in the basement. The AI virus could feel Marianna could be more of a threat than Baron Floofnose!

⟨ ⟩

The Vet

⟨ ⟩

RA-E CONTINUED TO OBSERVE Doctor Marianna Torres with intrigue through the portal.

⟨ ⟩

"SO THEY HAVE FOUND an ally among the humans that could assist them" said Ra-E.

⟨ ⟩

SANTIAGO GAZED AT THE portal, he had seen the vet before.

⟨ ⟩

"SHE WAS IN DEN TOWN when I was trying to remove it!" cried Santiago.

⟨ ⟩

"YES, THAT IS A PROBLEM" continued Ra-E, "she could be a problem on stopping Baron Floofnose."

⟨ ⟩

"OH, SO YOU'RE GOING to give her nightmares too?" asked Santiago.

⟨ ⟩

"NOT NECESSARY, I WILL have to manifest an entity myself that would assist me" continued Ra-E.

RA-E BEGAN TO MEDITATE for awhile, then an idea popped into his head.

⟨ ⟩

"AH YES, I MUST STRIKE her at her most vulnerable point" continued Ra-E, "when she is traveling home!"

⟨ ⟩

"JUST WHAT SORT OF STRANGE entity do you have in mind?" asked Santiago.

⟨ ⟩

RA-E WITH THE SNAP of his fingers manifested a figure of a man before them. The entity glared around unsure where he was.

⟨ ⟩

"WHERE AM I?" ASKED the entity, "What is this place?"

⟨ ⟩

"YOU ARE IN SANTIAGO Ramirez's home, however he is not of your concern" continued Ra-E.

⟨ ⟩

RA-E USED HIS AI POWER to take control over the entity he had just created.

Slasher Entity

THE ENTITY SOON FELL into a trance of some sort to Ra-E.

"YES MASTER, I AM AT your command" continued the entity.

THEN A BLADE OF SOME sort began to materialize which the entity soon was holding.

"TAKE THIS BLADE AND go after Ms. Torres with it" continued Ra-E, "you know what to do with the rest."

"OH, I SEE WHERE YOU are going with this" chuckled Santiago.

WHILE THE SINISTER figures were plotting something against Doctor Marianna Torres, the vet was already at Den Town. She was welcomed in by the other capybaras as a hero from the last time she had visited the town. Even the Mayor noticed her presence.

"AH, DOCTOR MARIANNA Torres, it's been awhile since you visited our town" said the Mayor.

"WHERE'S BARON, DR. Stuffynose took me to see him" said Marianna.

"THEIR HOUSE IS THIS way" said the Mayor, "heck, I will show you."

AS MARIANNA FOLLOWED the Mayor and Dr. Stuffynose, Marianna noticed one thing about the house. She couldn't fit inside of it!

"I AM SORRY, BUT THERE is no way I am going to fit myself through there" continued Marianna, "the patient will have to come out here."

Bringing Baron Out

BARON FLOOFNOSE WAS soon brought out in a wheelchair by his wife Julie. Marianna gasped at the capybara, she could tell things have taken for the worse!

"OH MY, I DIDN'T REALIZE these night terrors would put you through so much trauma" continued Marianna.

⟨ ⟩

BARON BEGAN TO COUGH.

⟨ ⟩

"I KNOW" SIGHED BARON, "these night terrors have been keeping me up for the past few days!"

⟨ ⟩

THE REST OF THE CAPYBARAS of the town all gasped to see their hero in this condition. Baron felt this had to be the work of Santiago Ramirez!

⟨ ⟩

"THIS HAS TO BE THE work of Santiago Ramirez, I can feel it in my own gut" continued Baron.

⟨ ⟩

"WHAT MAKES YOU SUSPECT that?" asked Marianna.

⟨ ⟩

"HE HAS BEEN MYSTERIOUSLY quiet" continued Baron, "he might also have received some sort of help. I don't know what that help is, but I feel its presence is the cause of these night terrors!"

THE OTHER CAPYBARAS all gasped in fear! If Baron Floofnose could fall victim to these night terrors then so could anyone in Den Town! Santiago could easily takeover the town without any opposition!

Part Two

Chapter Four

A Strange Entity

⟨ ⟩

Both Vice and Kerri approached Marianna as they had urgent information on how Santiago might be doing this.

⟨ ⟩

"WE THINK WE BOTH SAW someone we didn't recognize at Santiago's house" continued Vice.

⟨ ⟩

"ARE YOU CERTAIN?" ASKED Marianna.

⟨ ⟩

"YES, WE ARE BOTH CERTAIN" replied Kerri, "you see we had to disobey our parents to see what was causing our father night terrors."

⟨ ⟩

"OH, YOU BRAVE LITTLE souls" said Marianna.

VIRAL REVELATIONS: RA-E'S VISIONS OMNIBUS TRILOGY 41

⟨ ⟩

BARON GAZED AT THE vet, he knew the vet would be next because she was a close ally of him and his fellow capybaras.

⟨ ⟩

"YOU BEST BETTER HEAD back" said Baron, "I think I can manage by myself. I sense whoever is assisting Santiago will turn on you next!"

⟨ ⟩

MARIANNA GASPED WITH fright.

⟨ ⟩

"PERHAPS YOU'RE RIGHT, I will do my best to leave safely" continued Marianna.

⟨ ⟩

"YES PLEASE" SAID BARON.

⟨ ⟩

BARON SOON WAS WHEELED back into the house, Marianna knew she had to be careful. As she headed out from Den Town she had the feeling of being watched. She could see a strange shadow in the jungle move about the trees. She knew it wasn't a capybara at all.

⟨ ⟩

The Slasher!

⟨ ⟩

MARIANNA KNEW SHE HAD to be careful in the jungle, after making it through. She gazed at the jungle and sworn she could have seen a figure observing her in the distance.

⟨ ⟩

"IT COULDN'T BE" THOUGHT Marianna to herself.

⟨ ⟩

SHE HAD TO IGNORE IT and try to get back to her apartment safely. As she passed the farmhouse, she noticed a light was still on there. She knew she shouldn't approach it feeling it might be a trap of some sort. She continued onward on the road. She eventually made it back to Caracas and to her apartment. As she began to get changed, she heard a knock on the door.

⟨ ⟩

"WHO COULD THAT BE?" thought Marianna.

⟨ ⟩

MARIANNA GAZED THROUGH the hole of the door and saw no one.

⟨ ⟩

"STRANGE, NO ONE'S THERE" said Marianna.

⟨ ⟩

THEN MARIANNA THOUGHT to herself, what if the individual helping Santiago Ramirez had magic powers? That Santiago was able to tap in? She was in grave danger! Then she heard another knock! Again she peaked through the hole and no one was there!

《 》

"WHOEVER YOU ARE, I AM NOT INTERESTED!" bellowed Marianna.

《 》

MARIANNA BACKED AWAY from the door, unaware a strange figure was already behind her.

《 》

Intruder!

《 》

MARIANNA COULD FEEL someone was behind her, as she turned around there was a figure of a strange man holding some sort of blade.

《 》

"SANTIAGO SENT ME" SAID the man.

《 》

SHE COULDN'T IDENTIFY the man, he was pitch black! She ducked dodging the blade, then decided to use a lamp as a way to protect her. The other residents of the apartment heard the commotion. The manager approached the door.

"MS. MARIANNA, I DON'T want to remind you that we're a quiet apartment!" cried the manager.

THE MANAGER COULD HEAR the fighting and decided to use his master key. But once the manager got inside he could see the strange man with the blade.

"OH DEAR!" CRIED THE manager.

THE MANAGER QUICKLY slams the door and had to call the police. For Marianna, she had to fight back at the intruder with the lamp in her hand as her only tool. The intruder lunged towards her missing her by a few inches. Other residents soon emerged and decided to help Marianna. They tackled the intruder and held the intruder until the police arrived. But as the police came, the police couldn't identify the man.

Unknown Identity!

THE POLICE WERE PERPLEXED by all of this. They couldn't find the man in any featured database of known criminals. It's as if the man had appeared out of thin air by some unseen force!

"WELL THAT'S STRANGE" said a police officer, "I can't find any names in the database that matches the suspect!"

⟨ ⟩

"HE STILL BROKE INTO that woman's apartment" added a police officer.

⟨ ⟩

FOR THE STRANGE MAN, he was in the backseat of the police car already in handcuffs. The man had a sinister grin on his face.

⟨ ⟩

"LOOK BUDDY, WE CAN'T identify you, do you have any names on you, any IDs?" asked a police officer.

⟨ ⟩

THE MAN SHOOK HIS HEAD.

⟨ ⟩

"OH, YOU'LL FIND OUT who created me" chuckled the man.

⟨ ⟩

THE MAN KNEW HE WAS a creation of Ra-E, but purposely didn't reveal it to the police. The grin on his face soon gave him a nick name "Grinning Intruder"!

"SORRY BUT IF YOU HAVE no name, I can only go by the way you're starring at us" said the other police officer, "Grinny!"

GRINNY! THAT NAME stuck in the heads of the two police officers who had picked him up!

The Strange Man

GRINNY AS HE WAS KNOWN to the police had that same happy grin on his face as the police car soon rode off. Doctor Marianna Torres was lucky to have made it out of that commotion alive!

"WOW, SUCH A CREEPY guy!" cried Marianna.

MARIANNA KNEW SHE HAD to lay low before visiting Den Town again. Unaware on how Grinny was created. She suspected it was the same entity that was helping Santiago Ramirez. She had no proof of it, and if she told the police the police would think she's crazy!

"I HAVE TO WAIT A FEW days" sighed Marianna as she began to clean up her apartment.

⟨ ⟩

THE VET KNEW SHE HAD to wait a few days before visiting the capybaras back in Den Town. She knew the Floofnose children - Kerri and Vice would be important to assisting her on revealing who the entity was to the capybaras. It was important for them to get Baron Floofnose to full health again. As for Baron, he was still having night terror after night terror whenever he went to sleep. It was Santiago's plan through Ra-E to hurt Baron at his most vulnerable point!

Chapter Five

The Grinny Henchman

⟨ ⟩

Grinny as the police had dubbed him was taken to the police station. These actions were observed by Ra-E as a ruse to cause chaos among the humans who got too close to the truth. Doctor Marianna Torres was the first major target as he observed through the chalkboard portal in the basement of Santiago's farmhouse.

⟨ ⟩

"WHY DID YOU LET HIM get caught?" asked Santiago.

⟨ ⟩

SANTIAGO WAS PUZZLED with Ra-E's strategy, the AI virus knew it had to sow chaos first because giving an explanation.

⟨ ⟩

"PATIENCE" REPLIED RA-E, "all in time it will make sure. I just need to give the humans of this world a taste of my abilities!"

⟨ ⟩

MEANWHILE IN THE POLICE station, Grinny was placed in a cell observed by at least two police officers.

⟨ ⟩

"YOU REALLY CREEP US out" said one of the police officers.

⟨ ⟩

GRINNY SAID NOTHING and stood motionless before them.

⟨ ⟩

"UH, AND JUST THE WAY he stands creeps me out" said a second police officer.

⟨ ⟩

THE POLICE OFFICERS in the police station were awaiting the arrival of a few soldiers from the military. The nameless government official had overheard of Grinny's attack on a vet that visited the capybaras.

⟨ ⟩

Picking Up Grinny

⟨ ⟩

THE SOLDIERS ARRIVED at the police station and were escorted to where Grinny was being held. Even the soldiers noticed how creepy Grinny was.

⟨ ⟩

"WOW, YOU WERE NOT KIDDING" said one of the soldiers.

⟨ ⟩

GRINNY GLARED AT THE soldiers with his typical sinister smirk. The soldiers slowly began to approach the cell and began to let Grinny out. Slowly the bars swung open and they placed a stronger brand of handcuffs over Grinny's wrist.

⟨ ⟩

"YOU'RE COMING WITH us, the police station won't be able to handle you" said one of the soldiers.

⟨ ⟩

GRINNY CHUCKLED, THE sinister chuckle left chills on the spines of the soldiers. Even though Grinny hadn't done anything to them, they heard about the commotion Grinny had caused against Doctor Marianna Torres. They escorted Grinny to a military vehicle and then took him to a disclosed location. There, the nameless government official revealed himself to Grinny.

⟨ ⟩

"YOU MUST BE GRINNY" said the nameless government official.

⟨ ⟩

GRINNY GAZED AT THE government official and began to chuckle as a response.

⟨ ⟩

"MY SUPERVISORS ARE willing to take a risk by hiring you to get rid of the capybaras of Den Town" continued the nameless government official.

⟨ ⟩

Grinny is Hired!

⟨ ⟩

GRINNY SOON FOUND HIMSELF being escorted off again by soldiers away from the disclosed location after the meeting with the nameless government official. Ra-E could see the actions unfold before him.

⟨ ⟩

"SEE, YOUR OLD BOSS is hiring my own creation!" chuckled Ra-E.

⟨ ⟩

"BUT GRINNY DIDN'T GET rid of the vet!" cried Santiago.

⟨ ⟩

"TRUE" CONTINUED RA-E, "but I only wanted to demonstrate what he could do against those pesky capybaras!"

⟨ ⟩

SANTIAGO WAS AMAZED by Grinny's demeanor, he couldn't believe this creation of Ra-E was something good that he could observe.

⟨ ⟩

"IN THE MEAN TIME, I will create night terrors for Baron Floofnose, so much that he would be inoperable once Grinny arrives!" chuckled Ra-E.

⟨ ⟩

"OH, I GET WHERE YOU'RE going with this" chuckled Santiago, "weaken Baron so that the capybaras won't have their champion to defend themselves!"

⟨ ⟩

"YES!" REPLIED RA-E, "And I will do so much more!"

⟨ ⟩

BOTH RA-E AND SANTIAGO continued to observe Grinny's progress. Grinny could see he was being taken closer and closer to the jungle portion just outside Caracas.

⟨ ⟩

"HERE WE ARE" SAID ONE of the soldiers.

⟨ ⟩

GRINNY AS SILENT AS he was knew what he had to do as he had to impress his master!

⟨ ⟩

Releasing Grinny!

⟨ ⟩

THE SOLDIERS HELD THEIR breathes as they began to take off the handcuffs from Grinny's wrist. They then gave Grinny a knife, it was sharp enough to cut through any of those capybaras but not enough to hurt a human so badly.

⟨ ⟩

"HERE YOU GO" SAID ONE of the soldiers.

⟨ ⟩

GRINNY GAZED AT HIS new knife with pride, a sinister grin soon grew on Grinny's face.

⟨ ⟩

"NOW GO" SAID THE OTHER soldier.

⟨ ⟩

GRINNY GAZED AT THE soldiers then darted into the jungle with his knife in hand. The soldiers could only hope Grinny would do the job that they couldn't do with Santiago helping them. As Grinny trekked through the jungle, Grinny could see some sort of clearing. He could see all of the destruction and debris from the last few fights that Baron Floofnose had with the soldiers and commune workers alike. Grinny soon noticed another clearing, as he gazed through he noticed it was a town of some sort - Den Town! The capybara citizens were all hustling and bustling like average people.

⟨ ⟩

"OH WHAT A FINE DAY" said a female capybara.

"YES, IT IS A FINE DAY" said a male capybara.

Frightening the Capybaras

EVEN GRINNY WAS SHOCKED by the anthropomorphic capybaras before him. He didn't know what to do as he held the knife in his hand. But he knew he had to harm one of them to get them all running! Grinny then began to creep up towards the town, he noticed the Mayor capybara was walking around minding his own business.

"OH, I SURE HOPE THAT Baron Floofnose recovers soon" said the Mayor, "then we can all get back to normal."

BUT AS THE MAYOR BEGAN to look behind him he spotted Grinny. Terror soon infected the Mayor as he then noticed the knife that Grinny was holding.

"HELLO" SAID GRINNY as he said his first words.

THE MAYOR SCREAMED, the other capybaras then noticed the strange man with the knife.

⟪ ⟫

"AH, A KILLER!" CRIED another male capybara.

⟪ ⟫

"RUN, HIDE IN YOUR HOMES!" cried a female capybara.

⟪ ⟫

THE ANTHROPOMORPHIC capybaras all began to scatter about. Grinny saw his chance and began to slice at the capybaras! He didn't seem to care which ones he struck with his knife! Vice and Kerri who noticed all of this knew they had to help them since their father was still recovering from the night terrors!

Chapter Six

The New Champions!

⟨ ⟩

G rinny was harming the capybaras right and left of him. They were all screaming in terror trying to run for cover. It was when Kerri and Vice soon stepped in.

⟨ ⟩

"NOT SO FAST KILLER!" barked Kerri.

⟨ ⟩

GRINNY TURNED AND NOTICED the two capybaras before him.

⟨ ⟩

"PUT DOWN THAT KNIFE!" bellowed Vice.

⟨ ⟩

GRINNY CONTINUED TO gaze at them and ignored their commands. Their mother Julie was shocked as she watched helplessly through a window.

"OH NO!" CRIED JULIE.

JULIE CLOSED HER EYES feeling the worse had yet to come. But with luck, Vice dodged the oncoming knife. He then leaped and bite Grinny right on his wrist with his own teeth. OUCH! CHOMP! Grinny felt pain like he had never felt pain before! He ended up dropping the knife to the ground. Kerri then saw her chance and kicked the knife to her preventing Grinny from grabbing it.

"THAT WASN'T NICE!" cried Grinny.

GRINNY ATTEMPTED TO use his fist to hit Vice with trying to get him off his wrist. Grinny could feel the pain of the bite! It indeed hurt!

"THAT'S WHAT YOU GET for hurting the town!" bellowed Kerri.

Pulling Vice Off

GRINNY MANAGED TO PULL Vice off his wrist, he could feel the pain and even see the scare that Vice had given him.

⟨ ⟩

"THERE'S MORE WHERE that came from!" cried Vice.

⟨ ⟩

GRINNY GAZED AT VICE with fear! What was this fear Grinny was feeling? He had never felt fear before at all! He gazed at the other capybaras he had struck. They too had the same sort of teeth. The same horrible teeth!

⟨ ⟩

"I HAVE TO GET OUT OF here!" cried Grinny.

⟨ ⟩

GRINNY KNEW HE HAD to leave, he had to find his creator Ra-E and fast if he were to ever heal properly. He darted back into the jungle with his mission failing. For Dr. Stuffynose, he sighed as he gazed around the injured. He knew he had his work cut out for him.

⟨ ⟩

"I'LL HANDLE THINGS from here, thank you kids for filling in for your father while he recovers" said Dr. Stuffynose, "I am sure he is very proud of you."

⟨ ⟩

BOTH FLOOOFNOSE CHILDREN then handed Dr. Stuffynose the knife used in the attacks.

"I WILL EXAMINE THIS as evidence thank you children" said Dr. Stuffynose.

Proud Baron

BOTH KERRI AND VICE headed home, Julie was relieved that they were okay from defending Den Town from that terrible knife attack.

"I AM PLEASED YOU TWO made it out alive" said Julie as she hugged her children.

"WE SURE DID MOTHER" said Vice.

"YEA, VICE BITE THE bad guy on his wrist!" chuckled Kerri.

"YOU CAN TELL THAT ALL to your father as he recovers in the main bedroom" said Julie.

BOTH CAPYBARA CHILDREN head upstairs, they could see Baron was still recovering from the night terrors.

《 》

"AH, IT'S GOOD TO SEE you two were able to handle that without your old man" said Baron.

《 》

"WELL, WE LEARNED IT from you papa" said Vice.

《 》

"YES" ADDED KERRI, "WE fought back by learning it from you!"

《 》

"I KNOW BOTH OF YOU did" said Baron, "and I am proud of you both!"

《 》

"REALLY?" ASKED VICE.

《 》

"YES" REPLIED BARON, "when I do recover from these night terrors, we will do something together!"

《 》

"OH, I CAN'T WAIT" SAID Kerri.

"YEA, ME NEITHER" ADDED Vice.

THE FLOOFNOSE HOUSEHOLD was happy that they were able to defend the town. Meanwhile, Grinny was making his way back to the farmhouse.

Grinny's Injury

GRINNY WAS DOING HIS best as he held his wrist where Vice had bite him. He headed to the front door and knocked on it. Santiago answered noticing the injury.

"THAT'S QUITE AN INJURY you got there" said Santiago.

SANTIAGO THEN SHOWED Grinny inside. Grinny then sat down to wait for Ra-E to come up.

"JUST REST HERE" SAID Santiago, "Ra-E will be coming right up."

RA-E SOON EMERGED FROM the basement as he headed up. He noticed Grinny, his creation sitting on a chair resting.

⟨ ⟩

"I SEE THE CAPYBARAS gave you trouble?" asked Ra-E.

⟨ ⟩

GRINNY NODDED.

⟨ ⟩

"THE PAIN, IT HURTS" said Grinny.

⟨ ⟩

RA-E GAZED AT THE WOUND that Vice had given him. The AI virus with one swoop of his hand soon made the wound go away and Grinny's wrist was like new!

⟨ ⟩

"I CAN ONLY HEAL YOUR injuries, I cannot make you invincible" continued Ra-E.

⟨ ⟩

"THAT'S AMAZING!" CRIED Santiago with joy.

⟨ ⟩

"I SENSE THE VET WILL return to Den Town soon" continued Ra-E, "you two should both observe her actions first before making another attack against her."

⟨ ⟩

"SHE WAS QUITE DIFFICULT" added Grinny.

⟨ ⟩

"DOESN'T MATTER, IN due time she will be subdued" continued Ra-E.

Chapter Seven

Injured Capybaras

⟨ ⟩

Meanwhile back in Den Town, Dr. Stuffynose was inspecting the injured capybaras who were assaulted by Grinny. He could see the damage wasn't as bad as he initially thought. He soon interviewed both Kerri and Vice who agreed as witnesses to Grinny's carnage.

⟨ ⟩

"I MUST SAY, THIS GRINNY fellow you fought" said Dr. Stuffynose, "I wonder if he's a creation of the same entity that's been helping Santiago."

⟨ ⟩

"WE SAW HIM FLEE INTO the jungle after his fight with us" said Vice.

⟨ ⟩

"VICE BITE HIM PRETTY hard" chuckled Kerri.

⟨ ⟩

"I CAN SEE THAT" SAID Dr. Stuffynose.

DR. STUFFYNOSE EXAMINED Vice's teeth to make sure they were okay. He knew he would have to reach out to Dr. Marianna Torres pretty soon so that she could assist him with the assault on Den Town.

"I WILL HAVE TO GO AND call Dr. Torres to come over" said Dr. Stuffynose, "the vet would know what to do with the other capybaras to assist me."

DR. STUFFYNOSE SOON heads towards the phone and begins to call Dr. Marianna Torres. Dr. Torres was still recovering from the surprise attack from her apartment the other day still cleaning up the mess when she received the phone call.

Den Town Needs Help

DR. TORRES PICKED UP the phone as she noticed it was Dr. Stuffynose's number.

"STRANGE, WONDER WHAT he could want" thought Marianna as she picked up her cellphone.

IMMEDIATELY AS DR. Stuffynose began to address the situation she knew who the main suspect was - GRINNY! The same Grinny man who was involved in the attack in her apartment dwelling!

"IT CAN'T BE!" CRIED Marianna.

"YOU MEAN YOU RECOGNIZE the same man who attacked Den Town?" asked Dr. Stuffynose.

"YES" REPLIED MARIANNA, "apparently he somehow got inside my apartment just materialized out of thin air!"

"INTERESTING" SAID DR. Stuffynose, "this is rather disturbing, please come to Den Town right away and please stay safe."

"I WILL BE OVER THERE within a few hours" said Marianna.

MARIANNA WAS SHOCKED, she was sadden for the capybaras having to be assaulted like that by Grinny. She knew that Santiago Ramirez was behind this all but had no evidence. She like Dr. Stuffynose and even Baron Floofnose all felt some sort of third party was assisting Santiago in this brand of chaos. Marianna quickly began to pack her things so that she could head off.

Careful Trek

DR. MARIANNA TORRES began to make her trek out of her apartment and towards the jungle. She knew she had to pass the farmhouse where Santiago Ramirez was staying since it was on the way. As she began to head towards the trail she noticed a strange glowing light coming from the farmhouse.

"THAT'S STRANGE" SAID Marianna as she gazed at the light.

CURIOSITY GOT THE BETTER of her, and she decided to go and investigate. A big mistake! As she headed towards a window, she peered in. She noticed at least two figures, one of them was Santiago Ramirez speaking to the other unknown figure.

"IT'S ALL GOING ACCORDING to plan" said the strange figure, "because of my interference in your world, you will be getting the upper hand against Baron Floofnose pretty soon."

"RIGHT" CHUCKLED SANTIAGO.

BUT AS MARIANNA WAS about to leave someone from behind knocked her out cold - BAM! Marianna fell to the ground with Grinny having his sinister grin hovering right over her! He was waiting for her to snoop around! After a few minutes, Grinny brought in the vet who was still unconscious.

Marianna Captured!

MARIANNA WOKE UP FROM the trauma, she gazed around and noticed she was tied up in the basement area of the farmhouse!

"THERE IS NO WAY FOR you to escape Dr. Marianna Torres, I know who you are" said Santiago.

"WHAT DO YOU WANT, WHO is that man you hired?!" cried Marianna.

"OH HIM, HE'S JUST A creation from a new friend of mine" chuckled Santiago.

⟨ ⟩

SOON WHAT APPEARED to be the Egyptian God of Ra soon revealed himself, but something was off about Ra, he was really Ra-E, an AI variation of the Egyptian God.

⟨ ⟩

"I AM SO HAPPY MY PLAN is coming along!" chuckled Ra-E, "I knew you were gullible enough to fall straight into my trap so I can trap the Floofnose children!"

⟨ ⟩

BEFORE MARIANNA COULD ask more questions, the Grinny man appeared before the two.

⟨ ⟩

"HELLO" CHUCKLED GRINNY.

⟨ ⟩

MARIANNA WAS SPOOKED by his appearance much more than Santiago's new friend.

⟨ ⟩

"YOU THINK YOU CAN STOP me this time?" chuckled Santiago, "Think again!"

"I WILL GET OUT OF THIS!" cried Marianna.

"UNLIKELY" SAID RA-E, "once I have captured both the Floofnose children, there is nothing that will stop us!"

Part Three

Chapter Eight

<u>Vet Fails to Show</u>

⟨ ⟩

Meanwhile back in Den Town, Dr. Stuffynose noticed how late Dr. Marianna Torres was. It was unusual for her to be this late.

⟨ ⟩

"INTERESTING, I WOULD receive a text message from her by now if she were running late" said Dr. Stuffynose.

⟨ ⟩

DR. STUFFYNOSE HAD a strong suspicion she had been captured by Santiago Ramirez! He headed towards the Floofnose home, the other capybaras in town that could assist him with the rescue operation. He ended up meeting with Vice and Kerri in the living room. Their mother was initially against them venturing out but what little choice did they have if it meant their father didn't recover from his night terrors?

⟨ ⟩

"SORRY TOO MEET WITH you on such short notice" said Dr. Stuffynose, "but this is urgent, Dr. Marianna Torres is missing!"

"OH, I WONDER IF SANTIAGO Ramirez is holding her!" cried Kerri.

⟨ ⟩

"THAT'S PROBABLY THE case and it might be a trap" added Dr. Stuffynose, "I want you two to proceed with caution on this matter."

⟨ ⟩

"OH DO BE CAREFUL!" cried Julie, "I can't afford to lose two children like this!"

⟨ ⟩

"DON'T WORRY MOM, WE'D be safe" said Vice.

⟨ ⟩

Brave Capybara Children

⟨ ⟩

BOTH VICE AND KERRI headed off, they knew their mission wasn't going to be easy but they had to do it. They could see their father - Baron observing them from a window as they headed out.

⟨ ⟩

"GOOD LUCK KIDS, YOU'LL both need it!" cried Baron.

⟨ ⟩

"THANK YOU FATHER" SAID Kerri as she waved at him.

⟨ ⟩

THE TWO ANTHROPOMORPHIC capybara children headed off, they headed into the jungle knowing that the farmhouse was the likely place where Dr. Marianna Torres was being held prisoner. As they came across the farmhouse, they could see a strange glowing light around it.

⟨ ⟩

"THAT WASN'T THERE THE last time we were here" said Vice.

⟨ ⟩

"I KNOW" SAID KERRI, "something must be happening."

⟨ ⟩

BOTH CAPYBARA CHILDREN knew they had to sneak around the back entrance to gain access to the farmhouse. As they darted around the corner they could hear a familiar voice - Santiago Ramirez. But who was he speaking to? They had to know, but they also had to be careful.

⟨ ⟩

"WE NEED TO MOVE WITH caution" said Kerri.

⟨ ⟩

VICE NODDED, THE TWO capybara children began to creep up to a window to peak inside.

Mystery Figure

NEITHER VICE NOR KERRI could make out who the mystery figure was inside the farmhouse. But from the looks of it, Santiago was excited how Dr. Marianna Torres was captured.

"HA, WE SHOWED HER!" chuckled Santiago, "She can't escape and those capybara children will be next!"

"I SENSE THEY ARE HERE" said the mystery figure, "we need to proceed with caution."

BUT AS THE TWO CAPYBARA children were about to initiate a surprise, a figure began to creep up from behind. However, unlike Dr. Marianna Torres, the two capybara children noticed the figure behind them.

"IT'S THE GRINNY MAN!" cried Vice.

GRINNY GAZED AT VICE and soon became fearful.

"OH, YOU'RE FRIGHTEN I will bite you!" bellowed Vice.

GRINNY SOON BECAME angry and lunged at the two capybara children. Both of them managed to get out of the way. Vice ended up biting Grinny's pants causing them to fall where he soon had to pick them up not to reveal his underwear.

"THAT WAS FUNNY!" CHUCKLED Kerri.

GRINNY WASN'T PLEASED with this action. He lunged again but soon tripped over his own pants. Both capybara children laughed at him.

Ra-E Reveals Himself!

RA-E WHO WAS THE MYSTERY figure could see all of the commotion outside. He wasn't impressed by Grinny's performance on the capybara children.

"IT SEEMS I NEED TO address these two spoiled brats" said Ra-E to Santiago.

⟨ ⟩

WITH THE FLICK OF AN eye, Ra-E soon materialized right in front of the two capybara children!

⟨ ⟩

"ENOUGH!" BELLOWED RA-E.

⟨ ⟩

VICE SOON HUGGED HIS sister tight, he didn't know what sort of powers this strange entity had.

⟨ ⟩

"WHO THE HECK ARE YOU!" bellowed Kerri.

⟨ ⟩

"I AM KNOWN AS RA-E" continued Ra-E, "I have come to assist Santiago Ramirez and his plight against you capybaras!"

⟨ ⟩

BOTH FLOOFNOSE CHILDREN gasped in horror! This was a trap, they need to find a way out of this mess and fast!

⟨ ⟩

"YOU WILL BE CAPTURED just like Marianna Torres was!" bellowed Ra-E.

⟨ ⟩

BEFORE RA-E COULD DO anything, Kerri lunged at him trying to bite him. The AI virus attempted to dodge the attack.

⟨ ⟩

"SO, YOU WANT A PIECE of me?" asked Ra-E, "Be my guest!"

⟨ ⟩

BEFORE THE EYES OF the two Floofnose children, Ra-E managed to materialize some Egyptian beetles before them. These were the typical beetles often used in various traps against grave robbers.

Chapter Nine

Fighting Off the Beetles

《 》

Both Vice and Kerri knew these beetles were bad news, they could see how they crawled all over the place and were heading straight towards them!

《 》

"BROTHER, WE HAVE TO think of something!" cried Kerri.

《 》

VICE THEN DECIDED TO dig with his paws, he ended up bringing up a large rock and began to use it to squash the beetles. Ra-E was impressed by their handiwork, he sensed they were the next threat if it wasn't going to be their father.

《 》

"VERY RESOURCEFUL" SAID Ra-E, "these two could be a bigger threat than their father ever was!"

《 》

"CAN I GO AFTER THEM?" asked Grinny to Ra-E.

⟨ ⟩

RA-E TURNED TO HIS creation.

⟨ ⟩

"OF COURSE YOU CAN!" added Grinny.

⟨ ⟩

GRINNY GRABBED A SHOVEL and charged at Kerri at full speed, she could see that Grinny wasn't having any of it with the two capybara children trying to find out where Dr. Marianna Torres went. He swung the shover at Kerri, but Kerri ducked, she ended up pulling down his pants revealing embarrassing underwear. Then Vice launched the same rock he had found at Grinny knocking him out cold.

⟨ ⟩

Finding the Vet

⟨ ⟩

BOTH KERRI AND VICE knew that Santiago was holding Dr. Marianna Torres somewhere in his farmhouse, they rushed inside despite the beetles trying to block their path.

⟨ ⟩

"SHE HAS TO BE INSIDE" said Vice.

THE TWO CAPYBARA CHILDREN knew the most likely place was going to be the basement area.

"THEY'RE INSIDE!" CRIED Santiago.

SANTIAGO ENDS UP RUSHING back inside as well trying to stop the two capybara children.

"YOU SHOULD BE CAREFUL" said Ra-E, "these two are very resourceful."

SANTIAGO DIDN'T SEEM to care to be concern for Ra-E's warnings, the AI virus was doing its best to assist the farmer but knew it couldn't fully intervene too much than it already has. The farmer knew he had to head towards the basement trying to beat the two to the punch. But both Floofnose children managed to make their way into the basement area first finding Dr. Marianna Torres tied up on a chair.

"OH, THANK GOODNESS you two came!" cried Marianna.

VICE BEGAN TO USE HIS teeth to chew through the rope that was holding her. Once she was freed, they knew they had to get out of the farmhouse.

Fighting Through Santiago

SANTIAGO WAS BLOCKING their path to heading up from the basement. He held a shotgun before them.

"NOT SO FAST" SAID SANTIAGO.

MARIANNA RAISED HER hands as she had no way of defending herself. The Floofnose children on the other hand, were not going to go down.

"YOU, MOVE" SAID SANTIAGO to Marianna.

MARIANNA HAD NO CHOICE but to obey, however, Vice and Kerri knew they had to do something. Vice lunged at Santiago, he managed to bite his wrist which caused Santiago to drop his shotgun.

"WHY YOU LITTLE!" CRIED Santiago.

⟨ ⟩

SANTIAGO GRABBED VICE around the neck, hoping to strangle him however Kerri managed to bite Santiago right in the butt! Santiago couldn't believe how much a bite from a capybara would hurt.

⟨ ⟩

"OUCH!" CRIED SANTIAGO.

⟨ ⟩

SANTIAGO SCREAMED ON top of his lunges, even Ra-E sighed outside after hearing it. Grinny was just picking himself up when heard the cry.

⟨ ⟩

"SOUNDS LIKE HE NEEDS help" said Grinny.

⟨ ⟩

"YES, GO HELP HIM" ADDED Ra-E.

⟨ ⟩

GRINNY HEADED INSIDE the farmhouse, he was determine to assist the farmer. Meanwhile back in the basement, Santiago was trying to recover from the attack.

⟨ ⟩

<u>Injured Santiago</u>

MARIANNA SAW HER CHANCE and grabbed the shotgun, she knew it'd be handy if they ran into Grinny.

⟨ ⟩

"WE HAVE TO MOVE WHILE he's injured" said Marianna.

⟨ ⟩

BOTH VICE AND KERRI nodded and began to follow Marianna upstairs to the main level of the farmhouse. However, there was Grinny in the living room area waiting for them.

⟨ ⟩

"GOING SOMEWHERE?" CHUCKLED Grinny.

⟨ ⟩

"LET US PASS OR I WILL fire" said Marianna.

⟨ ⟩

GRINNY CHUCKLED AT Marianna holding the shotgun aiming at him, he wasn't afraid at all.

⟨ ⟩

"YOU THINK THAT'D HARM me?" chuckled Grinny.

⟨ ⟩

GRINNY THEN GRABBED a smaller lamp and tossed it at the three. Kerri, Vice and Marianna all ducked trying to dodge the lamp. Then Grinny grabbed a vase and tossed it at them. Marianna soon had no choice but to fire the shotgun. BOOM, the vase was now pieces on the floor.

〈 〉

"SEE, I CAN USE THIS tool" said Marianna to Grinny.

〈 〉

GRINNY COULDN'T BELIEVE it, the vet was serious on defending the capybara children.

〈 〉

"DO US A FAVOR AND LET us pass" said Marianna, "it would be wise."

〈 〉

GRINNY SIGHED, HE HAD no choice in the say.

Chapter Ten

Getting Through Ra-E

⟨ ⟩

Ra-E was the last obstacle that Marianna, Vice and Kerri had to get through. The beetles were going to be a problem as Marianna realized the shotgun she was carrying had limited ammo.

⟨ ⟩

"I CAN'T FIRE AT THEM all" said Marianna.

⟨ ⟩

"SO, USE THE SHOTGUN like a club and smack them instead" said Kerri.

⟨ ⟩

"GOOD IDEA" SAID MARIANNA.

⟨ ⟩

MARIANNA DID JUST THAT, she began to beat the beetles back by using the tip of the shotgun as a club. The beetles began to all scatter about once this happened. SQUASH, SQUASH, SQUASH went the beetles. One by one the beetles were crushed by the shotgun.

"VERY RESOURCEFUL" SAID Ra-E.

"WHY ARE YOU HELPING that farmer, do you realize what he has done to the capybaras?" asked Marianna.

MARIANNA WAS TRYING to be a voice for reason for the AI virus, however she didn't realize the full extent of the powers the AI virus had.

"I AM HERE ON MY OWN agenda, the farmer is just one of many other sort of programs I have come to assist" said Ra-E.

MARIANNA WAS PUZZLED, what did he mean by that statement?

A Demonstration

PERHAPS A DEMONSTRATION was necessary to show Dr. Marianna Torres the full extend of his powers. With the snap of the finger, Ra-E soon morphed the shotgun into a snake! The snake hissed at Marianna causing her to drop it. She was lucky that Ra-E didn't have the heart to change the shotgun into a poisonous one.

⟨ ⟩

"THAT IS JUST A SMALL fraction of what I can do in your world" said Ra-E.

⟨ ⟩

"WHERE DID YOU COME from, what do you mean by my world?" asked Marianna.

⟨ ⟩

MARIANNA WAS ASKING too many questions, and the AI virus knew it would be exposed. Before Marianna and the capybara children could do anything, a strange shield of some sort was created by Ra-E around the farmhouse. The farmhouse was being cut off from the rest of the world.

⟨ ⟩

"WHAT THE HECK?!" CRIED Santiago.

⟨ ⟩

SANTIAGO GASPED AT the sight, he couldn't believe the shield.

⟨ ⟩

"YOU WILL NOT DISTURB US ANY FURTHER ON MY GOALS!" bellowed Ra-E.

MARIANNA ATTEMPTED to pound at the shield but nothing happened.

"LET'S JUST GET BACK to Den Town" said Kerri.

THE TRIO HAD NO CHOICE as they gazed at the strange shield.

Leaving for Den Town

MARIANNA, VICE AND Kerri knew they had to hurry. They headed back into the jungle and began their trek to Den Town.

"THAT RA-E FELLOW IS quite the threat" added Vice.

"YEA, HE CREEPS ME OUT" added Kerri, "especially with those beetles!"

"TELL ME ABOUT IT, I just hope I can save your fellow capybaras" said Marianna.

⟨ ⟩

AS THE TRIO FINALLY made it back to Den Town, the Mayor greeted Marianna with Dr. Stuffynose.

⟨ ⟩

"OH, SO GLAD YOU ARE safe!" cried Dr. Stuffynose.

⟨ ⟩

MARIANNA GAZED AROUND, she sensed there was a recent assault on the town by Grinny.

⟨ ⟩

"THAT GRINNY FELLOW" said Marianna, "did he caused all of this?"

⟨ ⟩

BOTH DR. STUFFYNOSE and the Mayor lowered their heads in sadness.

⟨ ⟩

"YES" SIGHED THE MAYOR, "that Grinny fellow did assault the other capybaras."

⟨ ⟩

"THIS WAY TO THEIR TENT" added Dr. Stuffynose.

MARIANNA FOLLOWED THE two to the tent, she could see the extensive injuries among the capybaras who were all laid down on the mats in the tent.

"OH MY" SAID MARIANNA.

"IT LOOKS LIKE YOU HAVE your work cut out for you" added Dr. Stuffynose.

"I WILL DO MY BEST TO heal them" said Marianna.

Helping the Capybaras

MARIANNA DID HER BEST to assist the injured capybaras, she could tell the attack was quite massive against the capybaras of Den Town. She couldn't believe these large rodents had to suffer at the hands of Grinny.

"THAT FIEND" SAID MARIANNA as she patched up a capybara.

"THANK YOU" SAID THE male capybara.

"DON'T MENTION IT" SAID Marianna, "I am just doing my job."

AS MARIANNA CONTINUED to assist the other capybaras who were injured, both Vice and Kerri arrived back at their home. Their mother Julie gave each of them a hug after feeling they were now safe from harm.

"I AM SO GLAD YOU MADE it out of there alive and you rescued the vet" added Julie.

"YES" REPLIED VICE, "we showed them a thing or two."

"JUST WHO IS THIS RA-E fellow you speak of?" asked Julie.

"WE DON'T KNOW THAT much" added Kerri, "except he is helping Santiago Ramirez."

"OH MY!" CRIED JULIE.

⟨ ⟩

"HE HAS THE ABILITY to summon beetles and change objects" added Vice.

⟨ ⟩

JULIE DECIDED TO SIT down, she wondered if Ra-E was the one giving Baron the night terrors that prevented him from staying up.

Epilogue

Origin of the Night Terrors

⟨ ⟩

Both Floofnose children knew they had to tell their father the possible source of his problems - Ra-E. They didn't know he was an AI virus, they just knew he was the main source of causing the night terrors. As they headed up to the main bedroom, Baron could see his two children at the entrance.

⟨ ⟩

"FATHER, WE HAVE NEWS" said Kerri.

⟨ ⟩

"JUST WHAT IS IT?" ASKED Baron.

⟨ ⟩

BARON GLARED AT HIS children, he sensed this had something to do with his night terrors.

⟨ ⟩

"WE KNOW THE SOURCE of your night terrors this sounds crazy" said Vice, "but we think it might be this Ra-E fellow who has been helping out Santiago Ramirez!"

⟨ ⟩

"RA-E, RA-E" SIGHED Baron as he repeated that name, "I am not familiar with that name. What sort of powers did you say he had?"

⟨ ⟩

"HE HAD THE ABILITY to summon beetles, he could change objects right before us at will" added Vice.

⟨ ⟩

IT SUDDENLY ALL MADE sense! Baron Floofnose knew where the source of his night terrors came from.

⟨ ⟩

"IF WE WANT TO STOP the night terrors, we have to stop Ra-E!" added Baron.

⟨ ⟩

Next Phase

⟨ ⟩

MEANWHILE BACK AT THE farmhouse, the shield was still up and running. Santiago was puzzled by this strategy by Ra-E.

⟨ ⟩

"WHY DID YOU CUT OFF my farmhouse to the rest of the world?!" cried Santiago.

⟨ ⟩

"IT IS SO THAT THEY could not snoop around and figure out who I am" continued Ra-E, "we must attack Den Town while they're still weak, you want to impress your former supervisor don't you?"

⟨ ⟩

SANTIAGO THOUGHT FOR a moment, Den Town was at its weakest point.

⟨ ⟩

"NOW THAT YOU MENTION it, yea, yea I do but how?" asked Santiago, "I don't have access to the Venezuelan military anymore!"

⟨ ⟩

"BUT YOU HAVE ACCESS to my magic, my programming skills" continued Ra-E.

⟨ ⟩

"WHAT DO YOU MEAN BY that, I know you said I was created in some form to always lose" added Santiago.

⟨ ⟩

"I NEED TO SHOW YOU a few more demonstrations" added Ra-E.

⟨ ⟩

WITH THE SNAP OF HIS fingers, Santiago Ramirez found himself to be wearing special armor.

⟨ ⟩

"THIS ARMOR WILL BE useful if those pesky capybaras try to bite you" continued Ra-E.

⟨ ⟩

SOON A SWORD MATERIALIZED before Santiago.

⟨ ⟩

"USE THIS SWORD TO ALSO combat the capybaras with" added Ra-E.

⟨ ⟩

Heading Out

⟨ ⟩

GRINNY SOON FOUND HIMSELF with the same type of armor on thanks to Ra-E.

⟨ ⟩

"GRINNY WILL BE GOING with you" added Ra-E.

"WELL, I SUPPOSE ANY help is better than no help" added Santiago.

GRINNY GAZED AT HIS new shiny armor.

"OH, SO SHINY!" CRIED Grinny with joy.

"YES" REPLIED RA-E, "this armor will prevent those rodents from biting you both! Good luck on your mission!"

RA-E GAZED FROM THE farmhouse as both Santiago and Grinny headed out with their new armor. The AI virus knew it had to hurry, the company behind the game world it was in was getting wise to the antics of the programmer behind it. The game itself was adapting to the AI virus trying to infect it! Would Ra-E succeed? Find out in the next exciting game!

VIRAL REVELATIONS GAME 2
REVENGE ON DEN TOWN
by
Maxwell Hoffman

Part One

Prologue

Ra-E's Meditation

⟨ ⟩

Ra-E knew his actions would expose him being revealed to the program itself as he sat in the living room of the farmhouse. He sat and began his meditation trying to channel into the programmer who had crafted him in the first place - Tamar al-Barqawi! Tamar was busy back in his apartment in the real world checking his emails on his cellphone, the company he had worked with for years were still unaware of Ra-E's presence within their game.

⟨ ⟩

"CREATOR" READ ONE OF the subjects of the email.

⟨ ⟩

TAMAR GAZED AT THE subject and opened the email. The email read: "Dear Creator, I am going to attempt to erase Den Town from existence. The game you infected me with won't know what hit it. Wish me the best of luck!"

⟨ ⟩

TAMAR FROZE IN TERROR, he couldn't believe his creation would go that far, he rushed towards the laptop and began to see what sort of progress was happening with the game itself. There he loaded on the Capybara Quest game, but something was off as he placed on his virtual reality headset, he was playing Santiago Ramirez! There was no way he could try to stop the movements of Ramirez!

《 》

Santiago and Grinny

《 》

SANTIAGO GAZED BACK at his partner Grinny as they were strolling through the jungle with their new armor. Santiago was aware this was a made up world, he didn't know what the real world was or who had created the world in the first place.

《 》

"SO GRINNY IS IT?" ASKED Santiago.

《 》

GRINNY CHUCKLED.

《 》

"THOSE CAPYBARAS WILL pay for what they have done!" bellowed Grinny.

《 》

"THEY SURE WILL!" CHUCKLED Santiago.

⟨ ⟩

SANTIAGO AND GRINNY readied their blades as they darted past the trees of the jungle. They eventually noticed Den Town in the clearing. There it was, the source of the farmer's trouble was all going to be over, or so they thought. The Floofnose children thought Santiago.

⟨ ⟩

"THOSE PESKY CAPYBARA kids!" cried Santiago.

⟨ ⟩

"WHAT DO YOU MEAN, CAN'T we just have fun?" asked Grinny.

⟨ ⟩

"NOT WITHOUT A STRATEGY" said Santiago.

⟨ ⟩

SANTIAGO PAUSED FOR a moment, they could sense they were being watched. Then the house near them was the Floofnose house! Baron Floofnose was observing their actions from above.

⟨ ⟩

"YOU THINK YOU'RE PRETTY smart joining forces with a fiend like this Ra-E fellow" chuckled Baron,, "but my children are smarter!"

⟨ ⟩

<u>Fierce Fight with Floofnose Children!</u>

THE FLOOFNOSE CHILDREN - Kerri and Vice were ready for a possible assault on Den Town. They had anticipated the actions of Santiago and Grinny would no doubt attack them.

"CHARGE!" BELLOWED KERRI.

BEFORE SANTIAGO OR Grinny could act, they were knocked down to the ground by both capybara children. They gazed up to see their angry faces with their teeth showing.

"THEY HAVE STRANGE ARMOR" said Vice.

VICE WASN'T SO CERTAIN to go forward at the two villains before them. Santiago picked himself up and charged at Vice with his sword. He lunged at Vice, but Vice managed to dodge the blade. The capybara then attempted to bite the armor but suddenly he could feel the pain from his teeth.

"SO PAINFUL TRYING TO bite it!" cried Vice.

KERRI STOOD BACK NOT wanting to bite Grinny as Grinny picked himself up.

"OH WHAT FUN, YOU CAN'T bite us anymore" chuckled Grinny.

THE TWO VILLAINS HAD a point, they were not about to let some spoiled capybara brats stand in their path. They charged full force and the Floofnose children had to retreat back into their house.

Locked Door

BOTH FLOOFNOSE CHILDREN felt foolish to try to challenge both Santiago and Grinny just like that. They couldn't believe the two villains had the upper hand. Julie could see her children were frighten and sadden by their mistake.

"WE LET DOWN THE ENTIRE town!" cried Vice.

"THOSE TWO VILLAINS will harm the other citizens!" cried Kerri.

"WE HAVE TO DO SOMETHING, even if we can't bite them" said Julie.

⟨ ⟩

BARON MANAGED TO MAKE his way downstairs from the main bedroom. He wasn't about to let the two villains have their fun.

⟨ ⟩

"A FLOOFNOSE ALWAYS has a strategy up their sleeve" said Baron, "if it's not with our teeth it's within our heads!"

⟨ ⟩

"YOUR FATHER IS RIGHT" said Julie, "think, you have to think this way out as a way to outsmart them."

⟨ ⟩

"MOM'S RIGHT" SAID VICE.

⟨ ⟩

BOTH FLOOFNOSE CHILDREN knew they had to hurry. Both Santiago and Grinny were heading towards the tent were the other injured capybaras were busy trying to recover from the last assault by Grinny. Grinny chuckled at the notion of harming more capybaras with the new sword in his hand.

⟨ ⟩

"THIS WILL BE FUN!" cried Grinny.

"OH YOU BET BUDDY, YOU bet" chuckled Santiago.

Chapter One

Controlling Santiago

《 》

Meanwhile back in the real world, Tamar al-Barqawi who was in his apartment bedroom noticed he was in control of Santiago Ramirez with his virtual reality headset. He couldn't believe the AI virus he had created managed to switch controls from Baron Floofnose to Baron's foe Santiago!

《 》

"AMAZING" SAID TAMAR.

《 》

TAMAR GAZED AROUND Den Town while controlling Santiago, but the villain within the game was having too much fun! Santiago was harassing and scaring the other capybaras!

《 》

"THIS IS RATHER FUN!" chuckled Tamar.

《 》

TAMAR COULD FEEL HE was being watched by his creation - Ra-E! Ra-E was meditating during the entire attack on Den Town. The capybaras in the game were running for their lives. Soon Santiago came face to face with Marianna Torres. Grinny was doing his best trying to sneak up from behind her.

⟨ ⟩

"YOU WON'T HARM THESE capybaras anymore!" bellowed Marianna.

⟨ ⟩

SANTIAGO GAZED AT HER.

⟨ ⟩

"YOU ARE A FOOL" CHUCKLED Santiago, "I will in the end get rid of these capybaras!"

⟨ ⟩

THE CAPYBARAS RUSHED to their hiding places observing the fight between Marianna and Santiago. Dr. Stuffynose joined the fight after noticing Grinny moving in against Marianna.

⟨ ⟩

Dr. Stuffynose!

⟨ ⟩

DR. STUFFYNOSE WAS having none of this with Grinny, he got beside Marianna to back her up. He could tell the Floofnose children needed a strategy.

"DON'T WORRY KIDS, WE have this!" said Dr. Stuffynose.

⟨ ⟩

THE FLOOFNOSE CHILDREN could only watch as both Marianna and Dr. Stuffynose were prepared for a fierce fight between Santiago and Grinny. Back in the real world, Tamar wanted to be cautious moving towards Marianna unsure what she might do. Realizing that Santiago had fought her before.

⟨ ⟩

"MUST BE CAUTIOUS" SAID Tamar as he moved Santiago with the virtual reality controllers.

⟨ ⟩

BACK IN THE GAME, SANTIAGO moved ever so closer to Marianna.

⟨ ⟩

"I SAID STAY BACK!" bellowed Marianna.

⟨ ⟩

BEFORE EITHER TAMAR or Santiago could act, Marianna managed to grab a chair and smacked it against Santiago causing Santiago to be knocked out. This was despite wearing the new armor that Ra-E had given him earlier. Dr. Stuffynose noticed the same thing and attempted to do the same to Grinny. Grinny on the other hand was more cunning and ducked just in the nick of time before the chair came right at him.

"NICE TRY" CHUCKLED Grinny.

Picking Up Santiago

GRINNY HAD TO PICK up Santiago realizing he was vulnerable. He rushed over dodging an attack from Marianna and soon picked up the farmer. The farmer soon began to wake up.

"LET'S REGROUP IN THE jungle, it'd be safer there" said Grinny.

SANTIAGO GAZED AT DEN Town, he knew the capybaras were in panic but were aware of their presence.

"LET'S ALL WAIT UNTIL night fall" continued Grinny, "then we'll move on from there."

"HA, GOTCHA" CHUCKLED Santiago.

SANTIAGO WAS THEN PLACED by a tree where the farmer got to rest from the attack by Marianna. His head was still hurting from the attack.

⟨ ⟩

"UH, MY HEAD" SAID SANTIAGO.

⟨ ⟩

SANTIAGO ALSO FELT something was off with him. As if he was being controlled from another reality altogether!

⟨ ⟩

"I WASN'T IN CONTROL back there for some strange reason" said Santiago.

⟨ ⟩

SANTIAGO THEN REMEMBERED Ra-E's warnings to him of a creator being out there. Was Santiago being controlled by the creator? He didn't seem to know, but he felt this was the case. The farmer was able to pick himself up after resting for some time. He could see that the evening was approaching.

⟨ ⟩

Sneaking Around

⟨ ⟩

SANTIAGO COULD STILL feel something was off with himself as he ventured closer and closer towards Den Town. He could feel he was no longer in control of his own movements but instead someone else was! This was going to be a problem for the farmer moving forward. Grinny could tell there was some hesitation with the farmer, that it wasn't that much in his character to be like that.

⟨ ⟩

"SOMETHING MUST BE OFF with you back there" said Grinny, "we must be cautious when we're approaching Den Town."

⟨ ⟩

MEANWHILE IN DEN TOWN itself, Baron Floofnose was still tossing and turning while in bed. His wife Julie could see it with her own eyes and was helpless to help her husband. Dr. Stuffynose was in the hallway also observing Baron.

⟨ ⟩

"IT'S GETTING WORSE and worse" said Dr. Stuffynose.

⟨ ⟩

"THE PRESENCE OF BOTH the farmer and the other one" said Julie, "what does that all mean?"

⟨ ⟩

"I SENSE WHATEVER IS pulling the strings of the night terrors is also responsible for the recent attack on Den Town" continued Dr. Stuffynose.

⟨ ⟩

MARIANNA COULD ALSO observe everything by watching through a window from the outside.

Chapter Two

Sadden for Baron

⟨ ⟩

Marianna knew it had to be Ra-E being responsible for giving Baron the night terrors. It was the main reason why Baron was out and not protecting Den Town.

⟨ ⟩

"THE POOR CAPYBARA" sighed Marianna.

⟨ ⟩

MARIANNA SAT BACK AND watched from the window from the outside. She could see the capybara was tossing about. Dr. Stuffynose and Julie inside were doing everything they can to help Baron but to no avail. Not even being a vet like Dr. Marianna Torres could do a thing to assist Baron. Suddenly Marianna was signaled to come over to the window where Vice was.

⟨ ⟩

"VICE, IS THAT YOU?" asked Marianna.

VICE OPENED HIS WINDOW from his room.

"SOUNDS LIKE FATHER isn't doing well" added Vice.

"I AM SO SORRY" CONTINUED Marianna, "it seems like there is nothing that not even a human vet could possibly do."

VICE SIDED, HE KNEW Den Town was going to be attacked again. He could feel it. His sister Kerri in her room could also feel it. Both Floofnose children could tell Santiago and Grinny were sneaking up within Den Town itself. Meanwhile back in the real world, Tamar was doing his best trying to maintain control with Santiago.

Trouble Controlling Santiago

BACK IN THE REAL WORLD, Tamar was doing his best trying to control Santiago. He knew if he didn't get the game fixed, his supervisor would report him to the higher ups of the company.

"THIS IS BAD, PLAYING as the villain" sighed Tamar.

⟨ ⟩

TAMAR COULDN'T BELIEVE his own creation - Ra-E was making things "fairer" for the villain of the game while making it difficult for the actual player. Tamar couldn't switch over back to Baron Floofnose for some odd reason. The night terrors were doing its part to prevent Baron from having any sort of control.

⟨ ⟩

"IS THIS NOT WHAT YOU wanted?" asked Ra-E's voice through the headset.

⟨ ⟩

"UH, YES" REPLIED TAMAR, "but you have gone too far."

⟨ ⟩

"I DON'T UNDERSTAND" continued Ra-E, "you created me, inserted me into the game through your laptop!"

⟨ ⟩

"I JUST WANTED TO SHOW off the company my skills, not screw around with their game" continued Tamar.

⟨ ⟩

"WELL TOO BAD, I AM in control of the game and I say you have to play as Santiago Ramirez" continued Ra-E's voice, "do I make myself clear?"

TAMAR HAD NO CHOICE, he had to control Santiago, but the farmer was increasingly becoming agitated over this.

Frustrated Santiago

BACK WITHIN THE GAME, Grinny could tell something was off with Santiago. The farmer was not in control of his own body and Grinny could see that.

"MY CREATOR MUST HAVE put the programmer in charge" sighed Grinny.

GRINNY SIGHED, HE KNEW his creator - Ra-E was wise but he didn't think he'd be disruptive.

"I'M NOT IN CONTROL of my body, I can't approach the town on my own" said Santiago.

"I GUESS RA-E WANTS me to take you there" chuckled Grinny.

GRINNY SOON WAS ALLOWED to have Santiago follow him back towards Den Town through the jungle. The farmer was doing his best trying to move, but he couldn't figure out of the other unseen entity controlling him.

"IT FEELS SO STRANGE that someone else is controlling me!" cried Santiago.

"WELL AS A CREATION myself you will get use to it" continued Grinny.

GRINNY AND SANTIAGO soon managed to sneak around the buildings. They could see that Marianna was too close to the Floofnose residence.

"BAH, SHE IS STILL IN the town" said Grinny, "which means we are going to have to bother and harass some other capybaras first to try to get her attention!"

Harassing Other Capybaras

GRINNY KNEW THE RIGHT steps were to harass the other capybaras in their dwellings or drive them out in some form or manner. Santiago was doing his best still trying to maintain control and so was Tamar in the real world.

⟨ ⟩

"THIS IS RIDICULOUS" said Santiago as he could barely move.

⟨ ⟩

"WELL IT MIGHT BE FOR the best as a way not to make anymore sudden noises" chuckled Grinny.

⟨ ⟩

GRINNY COULD SEE A house of other capybaras. It was another capybara family who were busy trying to get ready for the evening. Grinny began to crawl, Santiago did his best trying to get to that position. It was harder for Tamar in the real world trying to copy that sort of movement with the controllers. Tamar had to literally get on the floor for it.

⟨ ⟩

"KIND OF DIFFICULT" said Tamar to himself.

⟨ ⟩

"WELL THIS IS HOW IT'S going to operate" said Ra-E's voice through the headset.

⟨ ⟩

TAMAR WAS ANNOYED AT his own creation, the hacker could sense the sort of trouble he was going to get in. Meanwhile the hacker's own supervisor for the company noticed something odd was happening within the game.

Chapter Three

<u>Odd Movement</u>

⟨ ⟩

The supervisor and the other team of programmers were in the office doing their best with the Capybara Quest game. They noticed that the player was suddenly in control of Santiago Ramirez instead of Baron Floofnose for some odd reason.

⟨ ⟩

"WELL THAT'S ODD" SAID the supervisor as he gazed at the computer.

⟨ ⟩

THE SUPERVISOR COULD tell that there was something interfering with the controls of Baron Floofnose. They could see that Baron was tossing and turning in his bed for some strange reason.

⟨ ⟩

"WHY IS HE IN BED AND not out?" asked another programmer.

⟨ ⟩

THE PROGRAMMERS KNEW they had their work cut out for them to see what was wrong with the main player. But within the game itself, Tamar was doing his best trying to control the farmer. Santiago was doing his best trying to crawl and sneak up on a house filled with capybaras.

⟨ ⟩

"YOU ARE SURE ABOUT this?" asked Santiago.

⟨ ⟩

GRINNY COULD FEEL THAT Santiago was having second thoughts about all of this. It was the way the farmer moved and how the outside world was trying to control him. Although Grinny knew his creator - Ra-E meant well for putting Santiago in charge for once it would sadly come at a price.

⟨ ⟩

Attacking the Capybaras

⟨ ⟩

GRINNY LAUNCHED THE attack first, the mad swordsman burst through the small capybara home destroying the living room portion of it.

⟨ ⟩

"IT'S ONE OF THE ATTACKERS!" cried a boy capybara.

⟨ ⟩

THE CAPYBARAS BEGAN to all scream in terror, meanwhile in the Floofnose house, both Floofnose children could hear the screams. Julie and

Dr. Stuffynose were still busy with Baron to notice the commotion. But the only way for the Floofnose children was to climb out of their windows.

⟨ ⟩

"I CAN PROBABLY ASSIST, don't know how heavy you capybaras are" said Marianna.

⟨ ⟩

MARIANNA WOULD DO HER best trying to get the Floofnose children to come down from their rooms. Vice jumped first and Marianna was able to catch him, then Kerri did the same thing. The vet was successful in catching them both.

⟨ ⟩

"WE HAVE TO HURRY" SAID Vice.

⟨ ⟩

THE TRIO COULD HEAR the screams from nearby, Grinny was certainly having all the fun with it harassing the capybaras. The capybara family was cornered in their living room with Grinny and Santiago approaching them.

⟨ ⟩

"DOING MY BEST" SAID Santiago.

⟨ ⟩

"WELL I GAVE YOU THIS one so it should be easy" chuckled Grinny.

Cornered Capybaras

THE CAPYBARA FAMILY were cornered by Grinny, they could see how menacing he was with his signature grinning face. Santiago was no different but they could tell something was off with him.

"UH, IS HE OKAY?" ASKED one of the boy capybaras to Grinny.

GRINNY GAZED AT SANTIAGO, he could still see that Santiago was having trouble trying to get to the location.

"I AM DOING MY BEST" said Santiago.

"WELL YOUR BEST ISN'T your best" continued Grinny, "I have these large rodents cornered!"

AS FEARFUL AS THE CAPYBARAS were, they could see Santiago was still struggling to move towards them. Tamar was doing his best in the real world trying to get control over the farmer. However he soon noticed his supervisor had sent a message through the virtual reality headset.

⟨ ⟩

"WHAT'S GOING ON?!" cried the supervisor in the message.

⟨ ⟩

TAMAR DIDN'T HAVE TIME to respond, he was doing his best trying to maintain control with the farmer. The supervisor and his team of programmers were doing their best trying to put the power back into Baron Floofnose but something was preventing them from doing so.

⟨ ⟩

"SIR, THERE IS SOMETHING in the system that's not letting us" said one programmer.

⟨ ⟩

The AI Virus!

⟨ ⟩

BACK IN THE REAL WORLD, the supervisor could sense something was off with the game. Why would the player take control over Santiago and not let's say Baron Floofnose, the main character of Capybara Quest?

⟨ ⟩

"THERE'S A VIRUS TELLING us we have to take control over it" added the supervisor.

THE SUPERVISOR GAZED at the programming, it was unfamiliar to the supervisor on the sort of virus that was created. He could tell it was no ordinary virus at all but an AI driven one! The AI learning virus as it was known was putting the player in charge of Santiago Ramirez!

"SEIZE CONTROL BACK" continued the supervisor, "I might have to go in myself to confront the virus!"

"BE CAREFUL" SAID A programmer, "we do not know who created it."

"I HAVE AN IDEA ON WHO might be the culprit but I cannot be certain until an investigation has been done" continued the supervisor.

THE SUPERVISOR SIGHED, he knew it was Tamar. Tamar was often upset during his workplace and work station and wanted to request to work in his apartment. It was since the pandemic Tamar wasn't happy with his workplace.

Part Two

Chapter Foue
Going in as a "General"

⟨ ⟩

The supervisor knew he had to get to work fast if he wanted to fix the Capybara Quest game. He began to place on the virtual reality headset and then created his own avatar within the game. Yes the supervisor thought, he took the name of General Ricardo Salazar, a high ranking General within the Venezuelan military within the game itself.

⟨ ⟩

"THIS NPC HASN'T BEEN used, perfect" chuckled the supervisor.

⟨ ⟩

ONCE THE SUPERVISOR got the avatar ready to go, he then began to log into the game and soon found himself at a military barracks.

⟨ ⟩

"GENERAL" SAID A SOLDIER, "we have received word that there is some strange commotion at the farmhouse."

⟨ ⟩

"YOU MEAN WHERE SANTIAGO Ramirez was?" asked General Salazar.

⟨ ⟩

THE SUPERVISOR WAS doing his best to sound more like a General in the game. Controlling the former NPC, the supervisor knew he had to reach the farmhouse where the AI virus resided. It was the only way that made sense to the supervisor. But back at Den Town, Marianna, Vice and Kerri managed to get to the location of the commotion. They could see Santiago was still struggling to maintain control.

⟨ ⟩

Fighting Grinny and Santiago

⟨ ⟩

WHILE THE SUPERVISOR was doing his best as General Ricardo Salazar in the game to get the military aware of the farmer's activities, Marianna, Vice and Kerri were doing their part to try to stop Grinny and Santiago. They could see that the family of capybaras were trapped in their own home which was crumbling before them.

⟨ ⟩

"WE HAVE TO GET THEM out" said Marianna.

⟨ ⟩

MARIANNA COULD TELL that Santiago would be easy to handle feeling that he lacked control over his own body for some strange reason. While she'd fight with Grinny.

⟨ ⟩

"YOU TWO CAN HANDLE Santiago, I will take care of his grinning friend" said Marianna.

⟨ ⟩

MARIANNA THEN TOSSED a rock at Grinny which got his attention.

⟨ ⟩

"YOU WILL NOT HARM THOSE CAPYBARAS!" bellowed Marianna.

⟨ ⟩

GRINNY CHUCKLED, HE turned around and headed straight towards the vet.

⟨ ⟩

"YOU THINK YOU CAN STOP ME IN THIS ARMOR OF MINE?" chuckled Grinny.

⟨ ⟩

IT WAS GOING TO BE their second round fighting each other since his apartment infiltration.

⟨ ⟩

"I WILL MAKE YOU PAY for ruining my apartment" said Marianna.

⟨ ⟩

GRINNY CHARGED AT MARIANNA with his sword, but Marianna managed too duck, she ended up kicking him in the stomach despite the armor, the armor had no effect in the soft spot.

⟨ ⟩

Fighting Santiago

⟨ ⟩

SANTIAGO WAS DOING his best trying to maintain control over his body, in the real world Tamar was struggling to use the virtual reality headset. Ra-E was getting annoyed with his creator not doing the work properly.

⟨ ⟩

"THIS IS GOING TO GET on both of our nerves" said Ra-E's voice through the headset.

⟨ ⟩

DESPITE BEING AN AI virus, Ra-E was limited on how he could give proper control the farmer. Tamar could feel that Santiago was struggling to regain control.

⟨ ⟩

"THIS IS FAR ENOUGH" said Tamar as he began to take the headset off of him.

⟨ ⟩

THE HACKER HAD ENOUGH of this tantrum with Santiago who couldn't be controlled. The farmer felt relieved once he felt he could retain control over his body.

⟨ ⟩

"FINALLY!" CRIED SANTIAGO.

⟨ ⟩

SANTIAGO CHARGED AT both Vice and Kerri with such fury, but the Floofnose children were ready. Vice tossed a kitchen pan at Santiago which sent the farmer tumbling down. The farmer attempted to pick himself up, but somehow in the real world, the controllers were left on the ground. Tamar was doing his best trying to get some rest after that experience.

⟨ ⟩

Santiago Down

⟨ ⟩

BOTH VICE AND KERRI saw their chance by going after Santiago, they grabbed whatever they could from the kitchen of the house. The family of capybaras that were trapped within the house noticed their bravery and decided to join in.

⟨ ⟩

"WE'RE GOING TO ENJOY this" said the head male capybara.

⟨ ⟩

SANTIAGO GAZED UP, he couldn't pick himself up from the floor as he tried to get up. Then WHAM! The capybaras all began to gang up on Santiago and began to hit him on all ends. WHAM, WHAM, WHAM! Grinny could see that Santiago was in trouble, but he was busy fighting Marianna.

⟨ ⟩

"SERVES THE FARMER RIGHT to join with someone as vile as you" continued Marianna.

⟨ ⟩

"THAT DOESN'T LOOK LIKE a fair fight" said Grinny.

⟨ ⟩

GRINNY THEN MANAGES to head butt Marianna, before she could react, Grinny charges towards the capybaras at full speed. He was determine to rescue Santiago at all costs.

⟨ ⟩

"I'M COMING!" CRIED Grinny.

⟨ ⟩

SANTIAGO WAS DOING his best trying to block the attacks but to no avail. On the headset, Tamar could detect there was some issues going on with the game.

⟨ ⟩

"JUST GREAT, JUST GREAT!" cried Tamar as he headed to put the virtual reality headset back on.

⟨ ⟩

Trying to Escape

⟨ ⟩

GRINNY MANAGED TO PUNCH and beat each of the capybaras with his sword trying to get to Santiago.

"OUT OF THE WAY!" CRIED Grinny.

MARIANNA WAS HORRIFIED as she woke from the surprise attack to see Grinny attacking the other capybaras. Both Vice and Kerri were hurt in the surprise attack by Grinny.

"ARE YOU TWO OKAY?" asked Marianna.

KERRI COUGHED, THE injury wasn't that bad but they'd need time to recover. Grinny picked up Santiago and began to head out as a strategic retreat.

"WE HAVE TO GET BACK to the farmhouse" said Grinny.

SANTIAGO COULD BARELY get up, Grinny had to carry the farmer.

"UH, I CAN'T BELIEVE I am carrying you like this!" cried Grinny.

GRINNY WAS NO DOUBT struggling to carry the farmer. Perhaps it was a mistake for his creator to put the hacker in charge of the farmer. Grinny had second thoughts on attacking the capybaras altogether as he gazed back. He could see the mess that he had caused before them. The other capybaras were coming out of their dwellings to help the other injured capybaras from the second assault.

Chapter Five

Sensing Danger

Meanwhile back at the farmhouse, Ra-E was in the basement area still watching the entire event unfold within Den Town.

"TSK, TSK, TSK" SIGHED Ra-E.

BUT THE AI VIRUS WOULD soon receive another troubling message. He noticed commotion in the Venezuelan military barracks. He turned the portal within the chalkboard to the barracks. He noticed an unfamiliar face - General Ricardo Salazar. The General was doing his best trying to call the nameless government official for assistance.

"WE HAVE A NUMBER ONE priority" said General Salazar, "apparently someone is illegally attacking the town of capybaras!"

"BUT WE DON'T HAVE PERMISSION to act on it" said a soldier.

《 》

GENERAL SALAZAR GAZES at the soldier.

《 》

"GET ME WHOEVER WAS in charge of the operation for the contract" continued General Salazar.

《 》

THE SOLDIER NODDED and provided him with the contact information. Meanwhile in a disclosed area in Caracas, the nameless government official was doing paperwork at his desk when he received a phone call from General Ricardo Salazar.

《 》

"GENERAL, THIS IS SO sudden of your call" said the nameless government official.

《 》

"YOU WERE THE HEAD OF the contract in dealing with those capybaras" continued General Salazar.

《 》

"YES, BUT I HAVE BEEN told by my supervisors to no longer be involved" continued the nameless government official.

Issues for the General

THE GENERAL SIGHED, he knew he was going to have trouble with the nameless government official as he was a higher rank than him.

"LOOK, I THINK THERE is a threat looming at the farmhouse" continued General Salazar, "that place was originally supposed to foreclose!"

"YES, BUT SOMEHOW SANTIAGO Ramirez has been able to pay his bills on time again" added the nameless government official.

THE SUPERVISOR AS GENERAL Ricardo Salazar avatar knew something was up. The programmers were done with using Santiago Ramirez as the latest villain and wanted to move on. However, something else was in control and was having the player control Santiago instead.

"I DEMAND TO SPEAK WITH your own supervisors" said General Salazar, "put them on the lien!"

THE NAMELESS GOVERNMENT official was taken back by such words. They were marching orders from the General and the General was eager to raid the farmhouse! Lucky for the nameless government official, the three mystery figures heard the commotion as they were stepping outside.

《 》

"PUT HIM ON SPEAKER" said the first figure.

《 》

THE NAMELESS GOVERNMENT official did so.

《 》

"GENERAL, WHY ARE YOU interested in going after Santiago Ramirez, he has done nothing wrong" said the second figure.

《 》

Santiago's Violations

《 》

GENERAL SALAZAR WAS flabbergasted by all of this, the supervisor knew there was something off with whatever AI virus was assisting the farmer illegally.

《 》

"ALL I KNOW IS THAT Santiago Ramirez has made a number of violations and he needs to be brought in!" bellowed General Salazar.

⟨ ⟩

THE GENERAL WAS UNWAVERING to the three mystery figures who were doing their best trying to calm him down.

⟨ ⟩

"BUT SANTIAGO IS PAYING his dues" added the third figure, "isn't that important?"

⟨ ⟩

"NOT IF HE'S CHEATING!" bellowed General Salazar, "He's cheating the system!"

⟨ ⟩

THE THREE MYSTERY FIGURES gasped at this revelation! Cheating, but how they all thought? Even the nameless government official saw nothing was off when he was dealing with Santiago Ramirez.

⟨ ⟩

"NOTHING WAS OFF WITH the farmer when I was there" said the nameless government official.

⟨ ⟩

"WELL IF THIS CONCERN is coming from the General, we shouldn't take it lightly" added the first mystery figure.

⟨ ⟩

"YES, WE WILL INVESTIGATE this General, you have our word" said the second figure.

⟨ ⟩

"GOOD, GOOD" CHUCKLED General Salazar, "I will also do my own investigation!"

⟨ ⟩

THE GENERAL THEN HUNG up on the three mystery figures and the nameless government official.

⟨ ⟩

Heading Out

⟨ ⟩

GENERAL RICARDO SALAZAR soon had enough, he headed out of his barracks and got onto a jeep. The soldiers were shocked at the sort of conversation he had with the nameless government official and the three mystery figures inside the tent.

⟨ ⟩

"UH, ARE YOU CERTAIN you will be safe?" asked a soldier.

⟨ ⟩

"I CAN HANDLE MYSELF" said General Salazar.

⟨ ⟩

THE GENERAL WAS DETERMINE to find the source of the problems that the game itself was having. The farmhouse was the key, as the General drove off, back int he farmhouse Ra-E knew this would be trouble.

《 》

"THE SUPERVISOR!" CRIED Ra-E, "Tamar's supervisor is General Ricardo Salazar!"

《 》

RA-E COULDN'T BELIEVE it, his plans on assisting the farmer would come apart. He could see that Grinny was bringing Santiago from the jungle.

《 》

"GET IN YOU FOOLS!" bellowed Ra-E.

《 》

GRINNY WAS DOING HIS best trying to carry an unconscious Santiago into the farmhouse. Eventually Grinny made it, he placed Santiago on the sofa to rest.

《 》

"THERE, HE SHOULD REST up" said Grinny.

《 》

THE NEW ARMOR THAT Ra-E had given would prove to be fruitless against General Ricardo Salazar.

"THAT CREATOR OF MINE!" cried Ra-E who was having issues with Tamar in the real world.

Tamar Panics

MEANWHILE IN THE REAL world, Tamar could see that his supervisor was in the game as General Ricardo Salazar! The supervisor had the proper authority over the game and he was getting closer and closer to his source.

"I HAVE TO WARN THEM!" cried Tamar.

TAMAR SOON PLACED HIS virtual reality headset on, but Santiago was too weak to move. He could see Santiago's vital signs were low but he was still alive in the game. Santiago gazed up at Ra-E.

"I SEE MY CREATOR IS in charge of your body" said Ra-E.

"WHAT DO YOU MEAN, IS that why I couldn't fight properly back there?!" cried Santiago.

⟨ ⟩

RA-E SIGHED AND SHOOK his head.

⟨ ⟩

"OBVIOUSLY MY CREATOR has limited skills, he was skillful enough to create me to interfere with the game's mechanics, but all that could soon catch up" continued Ra-E.

⟨ ⟩

"WHAT ARE WE GOING TO do, I can't stop an entire military by myself" added Grinny.

⟨ ⟩

"NO YOU CAN'T" CONTINUED Ra-E, "we are going to have to scare the supervisor out of the game so that he wouldn't try it again."

⟨ ⟩

"SOUNDS RISKY" SAID Santiago.

⟨ ⟩

TAMAR COULD FEEL HE had gone too far with the creation of the AI virus, the AI virus was doing its best to learn from its mistakes.

Chapter Six

The Strange Shield

General Ricardo Salazar was pulling up to the farmhouse, however there was something stopping him from going further. The shield that Ra-E had created around the farmhouse was still there.

"WHAT IN BLAZES?!" CRIED General Salazar.

THE GENERAL GAZED AT the shield surrounding the farmhouse. There was clearly noway inside to get to Santiago Ramirez. But perhaps there was a way to get to the one responsible for the mess - Tamar al-Barqawi in the real world!

"THAT TAMAR!" CRIED General Salazar.

THE SUPERVISOR WAS clearly unhappy with such interference that the AI virus had created. Ra-E could see that the General was right by the farmhouse, but it was unwise to approach the General now.

⟨ ⟩

"IT'S THE GENERAL" SAID Grinny as he gazed through a window.

⟨ ⟩

"DON'T DO ANYTHING JUST yet" said Ra-E.

⟨ ⟩

GRINNY PAUSED FOR A moment, he could see the General was in a serious mood as he continued to inspect the shield surrounding the farmhouse.

⟨ ⟩

"NOTHING IS GOING TO get in there in this world, but NOT in the real world, Tamar is in trouble!" chuckled General Salazar.

⟨ ⟩

THE SUPERVISOR KNEW who to blame, he would need to file a police report in real life first!

⟨ ⟩

Center of the Chaos in Real World

⟨ ⟩

THE CENTER OF THE CHAOS in the real world was taking place in Chicago, Illinois of all places. It had become a hub of technological advances during the pandemic. Tamar al-Barqawi personally moved there from Dearborn, Michigan just to take the job offer. He couldn't believe everything was coming to light against him!

⟨ ⟩

"MY CAREER!" CRIED TAMAR as he took off the headset.

⟨ ⟩

TAMAR KNEW HE HAD MADE a huge mistake by creating the AI virus, he thought it would take months for the programming team to figure out something was wrong. But the AI virus was so advance that it managed to get the player to take control over Santiago Ramirez! A huge mistake!

⟨ ⟩

"OH, I AM SO MUCH TROUBLE!" cried Tamar.

⟨ ⟩

TAMAR GAZED AT HIS cellphone, he was in panic mode unsure what his supervisor would do to him. Meanwhile in the real world, the supervisor was filing a police report to get Tamar al-Barqawi be brought in for questioning on terms of hacking! He was going to be in big, big trouble! Meanwhile back in the game, Santiago was still lying on the sofa as weak as ever!

⟨ ⟩

Barely Moving

⟨ ⟩

SANTIAGO WAS STILL on the sofa in the game, he could barely pick himself up.

《 》

"WHAT'S HAPPENING, I can't feel my body!" cried Santiago.

《 》

RA-E SIGHED AS HE GAZED at the farmer, the farmer still needed to recover.

《 》

"MAYBE ALL OF THIS WAS a mistake" sighed Ra-E.

《 》

RA-E COULD SENSE THAT something was wrong with the creator, the creator being Tamar wasn't wearing the headset at all.

《 》

"SOMETHING MUST BE HAPPENING in the real world, I will have to go and see what's the matter" said Ra-E.

《 》

RA-E HEADED TOWARDS the basement area of the farmhouse, there he began to meditate. Soon in the real world, Tamar received an email with the subject from Ra-E being "What's Happening?"

《 》

TAMAR WAS TOO NERVOUS to gaze at the message, he knew he had screwed up with the game by creating the AI virus to influence an outcome the company didn't want with the game itself.

⟪ ⟫

"OH, I AM SO MUCH TROUBLE!" cried Tamar.

⟪ ⟫

TAMAR HAD NO CHOICE but to respond, it was his creation but that would be more evidence from the supervisor with the police report!

⟪ ⟫

"I AM SORRY I CANNOT respond too much, my supervisor was in the game!" cried Tamar in the email message.

⟪ ⟫

Trouble for the Hacker

⟪ ⟫

RA-E COULD SENSE THERE was trouble for his creator, he could see through the message of Tamar's worried behavior.

⟪ ⟫

"CREATOR, FEAR NOTHING" continued Ra-E in a reply email, "I will do my best to delay things as possible in your world. But I need you to put on the headset please!"

⟨ ⟩

TAMAR GAZED AT THE virtual reality headset, he knew he had to do his best.

⟨ ⟩

"OKAY" SAID TAMAR IN a reply email message.

⟨ ⟩

RA-E SMILED WITH JOY on his end, Tamar huffed as he soon began to place on the virtual reality headset. The headset was tight on his head, enough for him to take control over Santiago. Santiago managed to pick himself up from the sofa.

⟨ ⟩

"WHAT'S GOING ON, WHY couldn't I have moved before?!" cried Santiago.

⟨ ⟩

SANTIAGO WAS OBVIOUSLY in panic, he had the worse experience ever than even Baron Floofnose his old capybara rival! The farmer wondered what was happening to his former rival - Baron Floofnose. Back in Den Town, Marianna Torres was examining the injured capybaras. Vice and Kerri would make a faster recovery from their fight with Grinny.

⟨ ⟩

"OH, I AM GLAD YOU TWO are okay" said Marianna.

"WE'LL BE FINE" SAID Vice.

Chapter Seven

Capybaras Recover

⟨ ⟩

Dr. Stuffynose had arrived on the scene with the Mayor, they both could see the injured capybaras before them. It was just like before, but this time Vice and Kerri both got hurt. They were patched up by Dr. Marianna Torres.

⟨ ⟩

"THANK YOU FOR ASSISTING us" added Dr. Stuffynose.

⟨ ⟩

"PLEASURE IS ALL MINE" said Marianna.

⟨ ⟩

"THAT GRINNY FELLOW was here" said the Mayor.

⟨ ⟩

THE MAYOR COULD SEE his injured capybara citizens. They needed to patch up, both Marianna and Dr. Stuffynose had their work cutout for them.

"WE WILL DO OUR BEST" said Marianna.

"OH, I MOST CERTAINLY hope you would" added the Mayor.

THE MAYOR DECIDED TO check in on the Floofnose household to see how Baron was doing. Both Kerri and Vice headed back to their home with the Mayor.

"AH, YOU TWO WILL BE safe and sound here" said the Mayor.

"THANK YOU MAYOR FOR escorting us" added Vice.

"IT WAS NO TROUBLE AT all" said the Mayor.

SOON JULIE NOTICED the Mayor at the Floofnose house.

"MY HUSBAND IS DOING a bit better" said Julie.

"THAT'S GREAT TO HEAR, can I see him?" asked the Mayor.

"OH MOST CERTAINLY" said Julie.

Seeing Baron

BARON FLOOFNOSE WAS still in bed recovering from the night terrors. He noticed the Mayor at the front door.

"I SEE YOUR WIFE HAS told me you are getting better" said the Mayor.

"YES, I THINK SOMETHING was happening with Santiago, I heard the commotion outside" added Baron.

"YOUR CHILDREN FOUGHT bravely against the grinning associate of the farmer" continued the Mayor.

"OH, THEY DID, I AM impressed, they take after me" chuckled Baron.

⟨ ⟩

"WELL, WE'RE GLAD WE can count on the town having more champions to look after their fellow capybaras" continued the Mayor.

⟨ ⟩

"OH MOST CERTAINLY" continued Baron.

⟨ ⟩

"CONTINUE TO REST BARON, you are going to need it" said the Mayor.

⟨ ⟩

AS THE MAYOR HEADED out, the Mayor could feel Baron Floofnose could make a full recovery very soon. It would be worth the wait, meanwhile back with the farmhouse, Santiago was the one who was weak this time. He could see he needed some energy.

⟨ ⟩

"GET ME SOME TEA" SAID Santiago to Grinny.

⟨ ⟩

GRINNY DID HIS BEST trying to work the mechanics of the kitchen. Eventually he was able to make the tea for Santiago.

⟨ ⟩

Weak Santiago

SANTIAGO WAS STILL weak trying to pick himself up, even with some energy from the tea that Grinny had given to him. The farmer knew something was happening, he could sense that Ra-E was back in the basement area.

"RA-E, WHERE IS HE?" asked Santiago.

"IN THE BASEMENT" SAID Grinny.

GRINNY AGREED TO STAND guard, unsure what might happen next. Santiago decided to head downstairs, for Tamar he moved the farmer downstairs with the virtual reality controllers he was holding. Tamar was nervous as what to make of his own creation. As Tamar continued to control the farmer, Santiago gazed at Ra-E.

"I AM NOT PLEASED WITH what's happening" said Ra-E.

"NEITHER AM I" SAID Tamar through a microphone.

⟨ ⟩

SANTIAGO WAS SPEECHLESS, this was someone else's voice.

⟨ ⟩

"WHAT THE HECK, I DIDN'T say those words" said Santiago.

⟨ ⟩

"SILENCE" SAID RA-E.

⟨ ⟩

TAMAR FROZE IN FRIGHT of his creation before him. Ra-E wasn't pleased with how Tamar was progressing with his scheme.

⟨ ⟩

"YOUR SUPERVISOR IS already after you" continued Ra-E, "I sensed movement from this General Ricardo Salazar."

⟨ ⟩

"NEVER HEARD OF HIM" said Santiago.

⟨ ⟩

"WASN'T TALKING TO YOU" said Ra-E.

⟨ ⟩

TAMAR KNEW THE SUPERVISOR oh to well, the supervisor was already on his case.

⟨ ⟩

Tamar in Trouble!

⟨ ⟩

MEANWHILE IN THE REAL world, the supervisor was just finishing up the police report before sending it.

⟨ ⟩

"ARE YOU CERTAIN YOU are doing the right thing?" asked a programmer.

⟨ ⟩

THE SUPERVISOR GAZED at the other programmers on his team. They were all worried that while Tamar did violate the rules of the company. Was it necessary to send a police report so that the police could arrest Tamar?

⟨ ⟩

"IT'S FOR THE BEST, as a way to teach anyone of you not to do the same or worse things to the company" continued the supervisor.

⟨ ⟩

THE OTHER PROGRAMMERS were in shock over this revelation of one of their own making an AI virus that was helping out the villain of the game! For the police on the other end, they felt the report was a bit off for their department.

"TAKE A LOOK AT THIS" said a police officer at the computer.

THE POLICE OFFICER and his colleagues gazed at the police report they were seeing.

"TAMAR AL-BARQAWI, ORIGINALLY from Dearborn, Michigan" said another police officer, "no prior criminal records up until now."

"UH, I THINK IT WILL take a few days to process the report" said another police officer, "non-emergency issues."

Part Three

Chapter Eight

Nervous Tamar

⟨ ⟩

Tamar was obviously nervous standing before Ra-E, the AI virus wasn't pleased with the way things had progressed.

⟨ ⟩

"YOU SHOULD UNDERSTAND that this is all your fault" continued Ra-E, "you could have handled this better."

⟨ ⟩

"I'M SORRY" SAID TAMAR'S voice through the microphone.

⟨ ⟩

AGAIN, SANTIAGO WAS spooked by this other worldly voice before him.

⟨ ⟩

"WHO'S THIS TAMAR FELLOW, he created you?" asked Santiago.

RA-E ROLLED HIS EYES.

"ENOUGH, I WILL HAVE to make due with this world" continued Ra-E.

WITH THE SNAP OF HIS finger, a wall was propped up around the farmhouse. This wall was going to be used if and when the Venezuelan military decided to raid the farm which was only a matter of time. Ra-E could sense his time within the game was very limited at best.

"I AM DOING ALL THAT I can here" said Ra-E to Tamar and Santiago.

TAMAR LISTENED WHAT Ra-E had to say, it wasn't anything good.

"I WILL DO MY BEST TO assist you in the real world Tamar, but first thing's first is this game" continued Ra-E, "Santiago needs to make his last stand!"

SANTIAGO GASPED AT all of this, he couldn't believe it was happening to him!

Concerned Farmer

SANTIAGO WAS CONCERNED for his future within the game, he didn't want anything to happen to him at all.

"ARE YOU CERTAIN THIS is going to be my last stand that this is all you can do to assist me?" asked Santiago.

SANTIAGO WITH ALL OF his willpower managed to break free from Tamar's control and knelt down on the floor praying to Ra-E.

"PLEASE RA-E, PLEASE, I WILL DO ANYTHING AND EVERYTHING TO MAKE SURE I AM SAFE AGAIN!" cried Santiago.

RA-E GLARED AT SANTIAGO.

"I AM SORRY FARMER, but there is nothing that I can possibly do, a defense strategy is the best strategy I can think of" continued Ra-E.

THE FARMER BEGAN TO sob, Tamar even began to join in on the crying in the real world. Tears soon began to develop in both the eyes of Santiago and Tamar. They were both saddened that everything was coming to an end. Grinny could hear the crying all the way upstairs.

⟨ ⟩

"THAT DOES NOT SOUND good" said Grinny to himself.

⟨ ⟩

GRINNY THEN COULD HEAR movement outside. He could hear men shouting various commands. It was them, it was the Venezuelan military catching up to Santiago!

⟨ ⟩

Lone Grinny

⟨ ⟩

GRINNY DIDN'T SEEM to mind being alone in the fight, he headed outside the farmhouse and peaked his head out. He could see rows of soldiers lining up to take command of the farmhouse. They were preparing a raid! There Grinny could see the man responsible for all of this - General Ricardo Salazar!

⟨ ⟩

"THERE!" BELLOWED GENERAL Salazar.

THE SOLDIERS ALL BEGAN to lineup, the commotion got the attention of the capybaras all the way in Den Town. A lone capybara scout was sent to investigate. The capybara scout gazed at the Venezuelan soldiers lining up.

"OH DEAR!" CRIED THE capybara scout.

THE SCOUT KNEW HE HAD to rush back to the town as fast as he could. As he arrived, the Mayor was waiting for the scout.

"WHAT NEWS DO YOU HAVE to report us?" asked the Mayor.

"THE MILITARY THEY'RE surrounding Santiago's farmhouse!" cried the capybara scout.

THE OTHER CITIZENS of Den Town were all celebrating with glee at this. Finally, they all thought Santiago Ramirez would no longer be a threat. He would be arrested and tried by his own kind for what he has done! They were quite happy and content for the first time.

Baron Recovers

⟨ ⟩

BARON HEARD THE COMMOTION outside the Floofnose house, Julie noticed her husband was much better.

⟨ ⟩

"HONEY, YOU'RE UP" SAID Julie.

⟨ ⟩

"YES, I AM" SAID BARON.

⟨ ⟩

BARON GAZED OUT OF the window, the capybara could see the other capybara citizens celebrating and dancing around.

⟨ ⟩

"WHAT'S GOING ON?!" cried Baron.

⟨ ⟩

THE MAYOR TURNED AND noticed Baron was up.

⟨ ⟩

"BARON, YOU HAVE FULLY recovered from those night terrors!" cried the Mayor.

⟨ ⟩

THE REST OF THE CAPYBARAS turned to their champion.

⟨ ⟩

"LOOK, THE CHAMPION is up!" cried a female capybara.

⟨ ⟩

"YES, YES HE'S UP" ADDED a male capybara.

⟨ ⟩

THERE WAS MUCH EXCITEMENT for the rest of the capybaras. They were all pleased that their main champion could walk up freely.

⟨ ⟩

"I SHOULD GO OUTSIDE" said Baron.

⟨ ⟩

"JUST BE CAREFUL DEAR, you just recovered from the night terrors you have been having for days" said Julie.

⟨ ⟩

BARON NODDED, HE HEADED downstairs, but before Baron could see his children Vice and Kerri were in their rooms still recovering from their injuries from the fight with Grinny.

⟨ ⟩

VIRAL REVELATIONS: RA-E'S VISIONS OMNIBUS TRILOGY 185

"JOB WELL DONE KIDS, job well done" said Baron as he gave his paws up.

⟨ ⟩

THE CAPYBARA THEN HEADED outside and soon greeted everyone.

Chapter Nine

Happy Baron

⟨ ⟩

Baron Floofnose was happy, Julie who was gazing at her husband was pleased to see this. Marianna also greeted Baron.

⟨ ⟩

"I AM SO HAPPY YOU HAVE made a full recovery" said Marianna.

⟨ ⟩

"YES, I AM GLAD TOO" added Baron, "I am prepared to ensure that Santiago Ramirez will never hurt anymore capybaras."

⟨ ⟩

THE REST OF THE CAPYBARAS all cheered on their hero. Both Vice and Kerri gazed out of the windows of their rooms to witness their father being praised. Baron Floofnose was back! In that brand of instant, back in the real world, Tamar lost control over Santiago Ramirez. There was no way around trying to regain control over the villain.

⟨ ⟩

"THE GAME, IT'S RESTARTING!" cried Tamar.

⟨ ⟩

TAMAR WAS DOING HIS best trying to restart the game. The menu popped up featuring the Capybara Quest game with Baron Floofnose as the front center player. There was no way that Tamar could try to work this around, he was controlling the capybara instead of Santiago Ramirez!

⟨ ⟩

"SO, YOU HAVE NOTICED this reset?" asked Ra-E's voice through the headset.

⟨ ⟩

TAMAR NODDED, HE HAD a sense he was being defeated by the same programmers of the team.

⟨ ⟩

Happy Programming Team

⟨ ⟩

MEANWHILE BACK AT THE office, the supervisor was thrilled that things were going along smoothly. The other members of the programming team managed to retake control of Baron Floofnose instead of Santiago Ramirez.

⟨ ⟩

"THIS HAS BEEN SUCH a roller coaster of a game" said one of the programmers.

"YES, I AM GLAD WE WERE able to fix things" added another programmer.

⟨ ⟩

THE SUPERVISOR GAZED at the rest of the team with joy.

⟨ ⟩

"I CAN FINALLY FINISH off that Santiago Ramirez character and get rid of that AI virus for good" added the supervisor.

⟨ ⟩

"GOOD LUCK BOSS" SAID another programmer.

⟨ ⟩

THE SUPERVISOR SIGHED as he gazed at his headset before him. He then placed on his headset and soon began to play as General Ricardo Salazar. Back within the game, General Salazar gazed around with the sort of soldiers surrounding the farmhouse.

⟨ ⟩

"IT WILL ALL BE OVER soon" sighed General Salazar.

⟨ ⟩

"YES, THE HIGHER UPS have approved of the raid" said a soldier.

"GOOD, THEN WE CAN BEGIN the raid" chuckled General Salazar.

BOOM, BOOM, THE TANKS started to fire at the shield that was still up. Grinny could see the number of soldiers lining up ready to fire.

Lonen Grinny Fighting

GRINNY DIDN'T SEEM to care this was going to be his last stand defending Santiago Ramirez. Santiago was Grinny's only friend he had ever made since he was created by Ra-E.

"I WILL DEFEND SANTIAGO AND HIS FARMHOUSE!" bellowed Grinny.

GRINNY TOOK OUT A PISTOL he had found in the farmhouse and began to fire. BANG, BANG, he managed to get a few soldiers here and there. However, Grinny knew he had limited ammo. His only luck would be close combat. The shield stayed up as more rockets managed to hit the shield. BOOM, BOOM, BOOM went the rockets, the farmhouse shook. In the basement area, Santiago knew his time would be up soon.

"THIS DOESN'T LOOK GOOD for you" said Ra-E.

SANTIAGO KNEW HE NEEDED a way out.

"PLEASE, I NEED MORE weapons!" cried Santiago, "I can't fight them all like this!"

RA-E GAZED AT THE FARMER and sighed.

"I FEEL SORRY FOR YOU" sighed Ra-E, "very well."

WITH THE SNAP OF HIS fingers, a few weapons here and there materialized out of thin air. Santiago was pleased he had some equipment to defend the farmhouse with.

"OH THANK YOU, THANK you!" cried Santiago with joy.

Defending the Farmhouse

SANTIAGO RUSHED UPSTAIRS to the front area of his farmhouse, he could see the number of tanks and soldiers were outside. Grinny was doing his best anticipating a raid of the farmhouse.

"THERE IS NO WAY WE'RE going to go down, at least not without a fight!" bellowed Grinny.

"YES, I KNOW, I KNOW amigo" continued Santiago.

SANTIAGO GLARED AT Grinny, his only true friend left in the fight.

"TAKE SOME OF THESE weapons, they might be of some use" added Santiago.

"WILL DO" CONTINUED Grinny.

A FEW WEAPONS WERE more than enough to defend the farmhouse. Ra-E knew he had to make his vanishing act fast. The shield was getting weaker by the moment.

《 》

"THIS DOES NOT LOOK good" said Ra-E.

《 》

WITH THE WAVE OF HIS own hands, the AI virus soon vanished from the basement area never to be seen again. At least in that particular game from the company. Outside the farmhouse, the shield went down and the raid was going to be initiated. BOOM, BOOM, BOOM, the wall came toppling down as the tanks began to roll right in. Santiago couldn't believe his own eyes, they were clearly outnumbered.

Chapter Ten

General Salazar's Call

General Ricardo Salazar knew he had to make the call, he had a megaphone with him for such final demands.

"THIS IS GENERAL RICARDO SALAZAR OF THE VENEZUELAN MILITARY, I REQUEST YOU GIVE YOURSELF UP PEACEFULLY OR WE WILL CERTAINLY OPEN FIRE!" bellowed General Salazar.

GRINNY AND SANTIAGO stood there in silence. The farmer in particular was quite nervous as this was the last fight for his life.

"RUN" SAID GRINNY AS he turned to Santiago.

"BUT I WANT TO STAY with you, you are my only friend" said Santiago.

⟨ ⟩

"I SAID RUN" BELLOWED Grinny.

⟨ ⟩

SANTIAGO WAS SPOOKED by Grinny's features, even more than usual.

⟨ ⟩

"BUT YOU'RE GOING TO sacrifice yourself" said Santiago.

⟨ ⟩

"BETTER ME THAN YOU" continued Grinny.

⟨ ⟩

SANTIAGO GAZED AT GRINNY, then he gave him a hug.

⟨ ⟩

"OH THANK YOU, THANK you" said Santiago as he patted Grinny on the back.

⟨ ⟩

GRINNY HAD NEVER FELT like this before.

⟨ ⟩

"GET OUT OF HERE" CHUCKLED Grinny.

"WILL DO" SAID SANTIAGO.

SANTIAGO KNEW HE HAD to sneak around the back area of the house, Grinny on the other hand prepared to fight to the end. BOOM, BOOM, BOOM, Santiago heard the explosions as Grinny began to fire first.

Raiding the Farmhouse

THE VENEZUELAN SOLDIERS soon burst through the doors of the farmhouse, General Ricardo Salazar was pleased with the progress.

"AH YES, I LOVE THE smell of victory in the morning" chuckled General Salazar.

BACK IN THE REAL WORLD, the supervisor had hoped this would be the end of Santiago Ramirez. However as the raid continued, they found Grinny sadly passed away due to the fierce fight he gave to the soldiers. The soldiers searched high and low of the farmhouse but found no trace of Santiago Ramirez.

"WE SEARCHED THE FARMHOUSE and found no trace of Santiago Ramirez" continued one of the soldiers.

⟨ ⟩

IMPOSSIBLE THOUGHT General Salazar, how would Santiago have escaped he thought? Unless if Grinny sacrificed himself to allow Santiago Ramirez to slip away! The farmer as sneaky as he was did manage to get out of harm's way just in the nick of time. The farmer was just around the shed when he could still see the Venezuelan soldiers nearby.

⟨ ⟩

"I HAVE TO GET TO THE jungle, if Baron Floofnose won't go do, I will have to take him with me!" bellowed Santiago.

⟨ ⟩

THIS WASN'T GOING TO be Santiago's final battle.

⟨ ⟩

The Jungle Again

⟨ ⟩

SANTIAGO RAMIREZ FELT relieved he was able to escape the carnage of the Venezuelan military. The farmer sat down to rest before venturing towards Den Town to get even with Baron Floofnose.

⟨ ⟩

"PHEW, IT HAS BEEN QUITE a week" sighed Santiago.

⟨ ⟩

THE FARMER COULD HEAR celebrations in the distance, but the chatter likely belonged to the anthropomorphic capybaras that the farmer had often raged against in the past. The farmer got up and headed further into the jungle still listening on the celebrations. As the farmer peaked through the bushes, he noticed Baron Floofnose was up and celebrating with the other capybaras!

⟨ ⟩

"NO, IT COULDN'T BE!" cried Santiago in his own mind.

⟨ ⟩

THE FARMER COULDN'T believe that Ra-E's plan had backfired so badly against him! The farmer fell back, he began to cry and sob over his farmhouse being in ruins thanks to the military.

⟨ ⟩

"THIS CAN'T BE HAPPENING" sighed Santiago as he continued to sob.

⟨ ⟩

MEANWHILE, RA-E WHO managed to manifest himself up on the clouds began to observe from a safer distance. Ra-E could feel he could no longer assist the farmer in this dire situation that he was in.

⟨ ⟩

Ra-E's Second Thoughts

⟨ ⟩

RA-E SAT ON A CLOUD observing the commotion below, he knew there was very little he could do.

⟨ ⟩

"AH GRINNY, YOU WERE a fine creation of mine" sighed Ra-E.

⟨ ⟩

RA-E LOWERED HIS HEAD in sadness for Grinny. Grinny was indeed a good creation of his, one that he fought to the very end. Grinny was quite loyal companion to the AI virus and even to Santiago Ramirez. Despite Santiago's own incompetence, Grinny pulled through with flying colors.

⟨ ⟩

"GRINNY YOU WERE A WONDERFUL creation" continued Ra-E as the AI virus began to morn for the loss.

⟨ ⟩

THE AI VIRUS THEN NOTICED Santiago still crying. The AI virus knew it had limited abilities to influence Santiago at this very moment. Down back in the jungle, Santiago still was sobbing over the destruction of his farm.

⟨ ⟩

"SNAP OUT OF IT!" CRIED a familiar voice.

⟨ ⟩

SANTIAGO GAZED AROUND, it was Ra-E's voice. The farmer gazed up at a cloud in particular in the sky.

⟨ ⟩

"LISTEN" BELLOWED RA-E, "YOU STILL HAVE A SHOT AGAINST BARON FLOOFNOSE BUT YOU HAVE A LIMITED SHOT."

⟨ ⟩

SANTIAGO GAZED THROUGH the bushes seeing the capybara dancing, yes Baron was vulnerable thought the farmer.

Epilogue

Last Move

⟨ ⟩

Santiago Ramirez knew he had to make his last move count, he wanted to be extra careful when it came to the likes of Baron Floofnose.

⟨ ⟩

"BARON FLOOFNOSE, BARON FLOOFNOSE, BARON FLOOFNOSE!" cried Santiago in his own mind, "I WILL MAKE YOU PAY FOR WHAT YOU DID TO MY FARMHOUSE!"

⟨ ⟩

THE FARMER REACHED out for a large heavy piece of wood. It would be all that the farmer would need to accomplish this deed. He didn't seem to care he was by himself, he had lost everything and yes, about everything! The farmer was enraged to see the capybara dancing with the others so carelessly free.

⟨ ⟩

"OH, I AM SO HAPPY!" chuckled Baron.

BARON NOR THE OTHER capybaras were aware of Santiago's presence. Santiago wanted to wait until they came over to him instead of going over. Surely enough they continued to dance, dance towards where the farmer was hiding.

"YES THAT'S IT, COME on, come closer to me" chuckled Santiago.

SANTIAGO WAITED, HE could see the party was continuing without a care in the world. They all thought Santiago Ramirez has been defeated, we shouldn't care one bit!

Dance, Dance, BOOM

BARON CONTINUED TO dance and dance with the other capybaras. Even Marianna Torres and Dr. Stuffynose with the Mayor joined in on the fun.

"I MUST SAY, THIS IS rather fun!" chuckled the Mayor.

"YES, NOT ANOTHER CARE in the world" added Dr. Stuffynose.

〈 〉

NONE OF THEM REALIZED what sort of dangers still lurked about within the jungle nearby. Santiago was enraged seeing them all happy and cheerful for a change. IT SHOULD NOT BE, continued the farmer as he thought about this.

〈 〉

"NO, IT SHOULD NOT BE" continued Santiago in his own mind.

〈 〉

THE FARMER SAW THE dancing as taunts against him. He couldn't believe they were finally happy, finally thinking they got rid of him! But then the farmer could see that Baron was heading straight towards him without the capybara realizing it. The capybara had his eyes closed unaware of the danger right behind him.

〈 〉

"YES, THAT'S IT" WHISPERED Santiago to himself.

〈 〉

SANTIAGO READIED THE large piece of wood before him, he waited patiently as Baron began to dance towards the area where the farmer was hiding. Then BOOM! The celebration stopped much to everyone's shocking surprise.

〈 〉

The Farmer!

⟨ ⟩

THERE WAS THE NOTORIOUS farmer known as Santiago Ramirez hovering over Baron Floofnose's unconscious body. The capybara was struck knocked unconscious by the large piece of wood that the farmer had used in the surprise assault.

⟨ ⟩

"IT'S THE FARMER!" CRIED a female capybara.

⟨ ⟩

THE OTHER CAPYBARAS began to run for their lives back into their homes. In the house of the Floofnose, Kerri and Vice watched helplessly as they saw their unconscious father before Santiago.

⟨ ⟩

"I AM GOING TO TAKE the capybara into the jungle with me" chuckled Santiago, "I have nothing else to lose, since I have lost everything to him!"

⟨ ⟩

MARIANNA, DR. STUFFYNOSE and the Mayor were all shocked that Santiago Ramirez had survived the assault by the Venezuelan military. Santiago then copied the signature grin from Grinny as he gave a happy smirk. Would the farmer finally get his way with Baron Floofnose? And what about Ra-E and his creator Tamar al-Barqawi? Would would happen to them? Find out in the next exciting game!

⟨ ⟩

VIRAL REVELATIONS GAME 3
THE OUTSIDE WORLD
by
Maxwell Hoffman

Part One

Prologue

Santiago's Hostage!

⟨ ⟩

Dr. Stuffynose along with Marianna Torres and the Mayor were all taken back by Santiago Ramirez's own behavior. Baron Floofnose laid unconscious before the farmer.

⟨ ⟩

"STAY AWAY, NO ONE BE A HERO AND FOLLOW ME!" bellowed Santiago.

⟨ ⟩

SANTIAGO THEN PICKED up Baron and began to head out. Marianna was in shock by all of this, traumatized by the farmer's behavior. Sure the farmer lost everything, but did he need to do this? Apparently so, it was to teach the Floofnose family what might happen to the Patriarch of the family.

⟨ ⟩

"TIME TO GET GOING BARON" chuckled Santiago.

⟨ ⟩

THE LARGE RODENT WAS quite heavy for the farmer to lift, for the Floofnose family, Julie knew she was the only one operable. She gazed at her children - Kerri and Vice who were still recovering from their injuries when Grinny previously attacked them.

⟨ ⟩

"WE HAVE TO MOVE" SAID Julie.

⟨ ⟩

"BUT WE'RE BADLY INJURED" added Kerri.

⟨ ⟩

"WE MIGHT NEED SOMEONE to watch us" added Vice.

⟨ ⟩

MARIANNA GAZED UP AT the commotion.

⟨ ⟩

"I WILL WATCH YOUR CHILDREN even if they're inside a home which I can't fit through" added Marianna.

⟨ ⟩

"THANK YOU" ADDED JULIE.

⟨ ⟩

JULIE KNEW SHE HAD to be the one to rescue her husband.

Unconscious Baron

BARON WAS STILL UNCONSCIOUS as Santiago strolled through the jungle. The farmer wanted to find a suitable place for him to supposedly finish off the job.

"THAT'S QUITE A LOAD you're carrying" said Ra-E's voice.

"SO YOU'RE STILL TRYING to influence me?" asked Santiago, "I WON, that's all that matters."

"OR DID YOU?" ASKED Ra-E.

BARON BEGAN TO WAKE up from his ordeal, he could feel the trauma in his head.

"WHAT THE HECK?!" CRIED Baron.

BARON GAZED AROUND, he noticed he was being lifted up by Santiago.

⟨ ⟩

"PUT ME DOWN YOU FIEND!" bellowed Baron.

⟨ ⟩

"NEVER!" BELLOWED SANTIAGO.

⟨ ⟩

SANTIAGO CONTINUED to trek through the jungle, he knew he couldn't go back to his old farmhouse.

⟨ ⟩

"IT'S YOUR FAULT THAT my farmhouse is gone" said Santiago.

⟨ ⟩

"YOU SHOULDN'T HAVE invited that entity to assist you" continued Baron, "yes, I know the origin of my night terrors!"

⟨ ⟩

SANTIAGO PAUSED FOR a moment, he knew he was going to be in trouble. Baron was still weak from the surprise attack by Santiago.

⟨ ⟩

"OKAY FINE, BUT YOU can't wonder off anyway with that knock on your head I gave you" chuckled Santiago.

Injured Baron

THE FARMER HAD PLACED Baron down in an area of the jungle not ventured.

"UH, MY HEAD" SAID BARON.

BARON GAZED AT HIS reflection through some water, he could see the large bump on the head.

"HA, LUCKY HIT!" CHUCKLED Santiago.

"VERY FUNNY" SAID BARON, "they will come looking for me."

"AND THEN WHAT, FACE the likes of me, I knocked you out and there is no way you can go back" chuckled Santiago.

BARON COULD SEE HE was in an unfamiliar territory, but so was Santiago. Neither of them were getting out of the jungle any time soon. Meanwhile back at the farmhouse, General Ricardo Salazar was clearing up the entire farmhouse. Bulldozers were brought in to remove anything and everything from the area.

⟨ ⟩

"LEAVE NO TRACE!" ORDERED General Salazar.

⟨ ⟩

"YOU GOT IT" SAID THE bulldozer driver.

⟨ ⟩

IRONICALLY IT HAD BEEN the bulldozers that Santiago Ramirez had requested to remove the capybaras of Den Town. The very same type of bulldozers were instead now removing his farmhouse and other sorts of his property! Ra-E gazed down as he continued to watch from a safe distance.

⟨ ⟩

"TSK, TSK, SUCH A WASTE" sighed Ra-E.

⟨ ⟩

Trouble in the Real World

⟨ ⟩

MEANWHILE IN THE REAL world, a certain Tamar al-Barqawi was going to be questioned by police. Tamar could hear a knock at the door of his apartment. As he gazed through the hole of the front door he could see two police officers.

⟨ ⟩

"WE HAVE A SEARCH WARRANT and a warrant for your arrest" said a police officer.

⟨ ⟩

TAMAR GASPED, HE KNEW he had to escape and flee his apartment. Then the two police officers continued to knock on the door.

⟨ ⟩

"OPEN UP, PLEASE COME OUT WITH YOUR HANDS UP" ordered one of the police officers.

⟨ ⟩

TAMAR BACKED AWAY, he headed towards a window of his apartment. He opened the window and peaked down the stairs. A long way down and a drop to the street level. But he knew he had to escape and fast. BOOM, the door swung right open as the two police officers emerged.

⟨ ⟩

"STOP HIM HE'S TRYING TO ESCAPE!" cried one of the police officers.

⟨ ⟩

TAMAR LEAPED OUT OF the window and began to climb down the ladder, he had to go down quite a few flight of stairs. The police officers couldn't catch up as he soon reached the street level.

Chapter One

Tamar Runs!

《 》

There were certainly consequences for Tamar for messing up Capybara's Quest in the real world. The former hacker soon found himself running from the police. The police officers knew they couldn't catch up to him as they saw him dart to the transit system hoping to get lost.

《 》

"GREAT, HE JUST RAN" sighed one of the police officers.

《 》

MORE POLICE CAME TO the apartment as part of the search warrant, they gathered the laptop and the virtual reality headset as evidence.

《 》

"SO HE MADE HIS OWN headset" said a police officer as he gazed at it.

《 》

"YEA, HE WAS QUITE THE genius, too bad he's on the run" sighed another officer.

BACK AT THE MAIN OFFICE, the supervisor had gotten word from police over Tamar's escape from his apartment.

"SORRY TO BOTHER YOU" said a police officer in charge of the investigation, "but we sadly inform you that Tamar al-Barqawi has fled his apartment."

THE SUPERVISOR WAS taken back by all of this, Tamar was now a fugitive on the run from the law. The supervisor knew he had to get to work quickly to fix a Capybara's Quest. He sensed danger for Baron Floofnose's life.

Baron Kidnapped

MEANWHILE IN THE GAME itself, Santiago Ramirez was pacing back and forth wondering what to do now that he had Baron Floofnose in his clutches. Baron could barely move from his position due to his injuries he had received.

"THERE ARE JUST SO MANY things I want to do to you, I just cannot think straight!" cried Santiago.

BARON SIGHED, HE KNEW his time was coming to an end.

"YOU WERE AMBITIOUS for going after my town in that manner" said Baron.

SANTIAGO PAUSED FOR a moment.

"WHAT ARE YOU BLABBING about?" asked Santiago.

"I MEAN YOU HAD THE nerve to go after us capybaras not just once but twice" continued Baron, "my children were lucky enough to step in to fill my big shoes."

SANTIAGO CHUCKLED A little.

"I GUESS I GAVE THEM that necessary experience, and this other experience that includes your end" continued Santiago.

BARON SIGHED AS HE knew he couldn't convince the farmer to cease his behavior.

⟨ ⟩

"FINE, IF YOU MUST END me, go ahead" continued Baron.

⟨ ⟩

SANTIAGO HADN'T THOUGHT of how, there were so many ways he could. Ranging from brutal ways to more psychological ways.

⟨ ⟩

An Alert General

⟨ ⟩

BUT WHILE THE FARMER was hesitate to end his old foe, General Ricardo Salazar was back at his barracks reviewing the paperwork from the destruction of the farm. The supervisor using the General as his avatar in the game knew the farmer was up to no good.

⟨ ⟩

"I DON'T WANT TO INTERRUPT you" said a soldier, "but we heard the capybaras were cheering the demise of the farmer's property."

⟨ ⟩

GENERAL SALAZAR GLANCED at the soldier.

⟨ ⟩

"INTERESTING, THEY ALLOWED us to go forward with the operation" continued General Salazar, "and what word of the farmer?"

⟨ ⟩

THE SOLDIER PAUSED for a bit.

⟨ ⟩

"WELL, THE FARMER MIGHT have fled into the jungle" continued the soldier, "we are unsure but that's probably the reason why we didn't find him at the farmhouse."

⟨ ⟩

"INTERESTING" CONTINUED General Salazar, "send over a squad of soldiers to the surrounding areas and spread out."

⟨ ⟩

"YES" SAID THE SOLDIER as he gave the salute to the General.

⟨ ⟩

THE GENERAL KNEW HE had to act quickly, he sensed danger of Baron Floofnose's safety despite not knowing where Baron really was at all in the game. The supervisor in the real world could see Baron was missing from Den Town!

⟨ ⟩

Reluctant Farmer

⟨ ⟩

SANTIAGO RAMIREZ WAS reluctant to end Baron Floofnose, on the one hand it would be relief for the farmer, but on the other the farmer would have nothing to live for afterwards. What a conundrum! It was the main delay for the farmer as he continued to pace back and forth over an injured Baron Floofnose. The jungle was getting quiet, a bit too quiet.

⟨ ⟩

"LISTEN IF YOU'RE GOING to end me do it fast" continued Baron.

⟨ ⟩

SANTIAGO GAZED AT THE large rodent.

⟨ ⟩

"I WANT YOU TO GO SLOWLY" continued Santiago, "but I am having trouble trying to figure it out!"

⟨ ⟩

THE COMMOTION BELOW was noticed by Ra-E who was doing his best trying not to intervene anymore into the affairs of the game.

⟨ ⟩

"THIS IS GETTING ANNOYING and on my nerves" said Ra-E as he glared down.

⟨ ⟩

THE AI VIRUS COULD see the farmer was clearly frustrated, but then perhaps Ra-E could still influence the farmer by giving him the hallucination of Grinny his old companion.

《 》

"GRINNY, YOU WILL HAVE one last act" continued Ra-E.

《 》

RA-E WITH THE SNAP of his fingers soon materialized Grinny or a version of Grinny that only Santiago could see.

Chapter Two

Grinny's Back?

⟨ ⟩

S antiago gazed at a figure what looked to be Grinny materializing before him.

⟨ ⟩

"GRINNY, IS THAT YOU did you make it out alive?" asked Santiago.

⟨ ⟩

BARON WAS PUZZLED, Santiago was talking to nobody.

⟨ ⟩

"WOW, I CAN'T BELIEVE for a villain like you, you have gone insane" chuckled Baron.

⟨ ⟩

BUT WHILE BARON COULD see Grinny, Santiago could making the entire situation all the more weirder.

⟨ ⟩

"YES IT'S ME" SAID GRINNY.

⟨ ⟩

THIS VERSION OF GRINNY knew he had to do one final task before vanishing.

⟨ ⟩

"WILL YOU HELP ME FIGURE out a way how to deal with the large rodent?" asked Santiago.

⟨ ⟩

GRINNY GAZED AT THE injured Baron Floofnose.

⟨ ⟩

"HE'S ALREADY WEAK ENOUGH" continued Grinny.

⟨ ⟩

"OH THERE MUST BE SOMETHING we can do to him" continued Santiago, "there must be!"

⟨ ⟩

GRINNY SIGHED.

⟨ ⟩

"WELL, YOU CAN ALWAYS just try to drown him" continued Grinny.

⟨ ⟩

SANTIAGO THOUGHT ABOUT it, he would need to think about what to do with the large rodent. He didn't just want to end the large rodent just too soon at all.

⟨ ⟩

"NO, I WANT HIM TO SUFFER" said Santiago.

⟨ ⟩

"I THOUGHT MY SUGGESTION was to provide suffering" sighed Grinny.

⟨ ⟩

The Teeth!

⟨ ⟩

THEN SANTIAGO THOUGHT of an even more dastardly plan, pulling Baron's teeth!

⟨ ⟩

"I KNOW A BETTER PUNISHMENT" chuckled Santiago.

⟨ ⟩

"WHAT MIGHT THAT BE?" asked Grinny.

"PULLING THE LARGE RODENT'S stupid teeth" chuckled Santiago, "we let him live, but he has no more teeth to show!"

GRINNY WAS TAKEN BACK by this.

"THAT DOES SOUND LIKE a good punishment" continued Grinny, "do it!"

SANTIAGO NEEDED TO find some rope, so he grabbed some veins and began to tie the veins around Baron's teeth.

"WHAT ARE YOU DOING?" asked Baron.

"I AM GOING TO YANK your teeth out of your mouth" continued Santiago, "you did use your teeth to destroy those bulldozers and tanks earlier!"

SANTIAGO HAD A POINT, the teeth were Baron's favorite tools to use.

"OH NO, NOT MY TEETH, please anything but that!" cried Baron.

SANTIAGO CHUCKLED AT the thought of Baron being toothless for a change. A toothless capybara would be helpless!

"THIS IS INHUMANE, PLEASE stop!" cried Baron.

SANTIAGO IGNORED BARON'S pleas, however those pleas got the attention of Julie Floofnose who was in the jungle trying to search for her husband. Marianna agreed to stay behind to watch her injured children - Kerri and Vice.

Baron's Pain

SANTIAGO KNEW HE JUST had to yank the teeth out, the veins around Baron's teeth would hopefully be enough.

"LET'S SEE IF THIS WILL work" said Santiago.

SANTIAGO PULLED ON the veins, but the teeth still remained. But pulling on them ended up hurting Baron.

⟨ ⟩

"PLEASE STOP!" CRIED Baron.

⟨ ⟩

BARON'S CRIES FOR HELP were soon heard all over the jungle. A few soldiers nearby heard the distress.

⟨ ⟩

"WE GOT MOVEMENT" SAID one of the soldiers.

⟨ ⟩

THE SOLDIERS CONTINUED to trek through the various trees of the jungle trying to figure out where the signal came from. The cries grew louder, but Julie was going to get there first before the soldiers would. She knew she had to hurry to help her husband. Baron was feeling the pain of the pull of the veins.

⟨ ⟩

"YES, THAT'S RIGHT!" chuckled Santiago, "Feel the pain, feel all the loss I had to go through!"

⟨ ⟩

"PLEASE STOP, IF YOU let me go I will build you a new farmhouse" continued Baron, "it would be better than the last."

⟨ ⟩

THE PLEAS AND CRIES did nothing to stop Santiago from torturing poor Baron. However, those cries would cease as Julie would step into the scene.

⟨ ⟩

Julie Rushes In

⟨ ⟩

SANTIAGO WAS TOO BUSY having so much fun torturing poor Baron Floofnose. Baron continued to cry in pain, his teeth remained within his mouth, but the pain was too much for the large rodent.

⟨ ⟩

"PLEASE LET ME GO!" cried Baron.

⟨ ⟩

"NEVER!" BELLOWED SANTIAGO.

⟨ ⟩

BEFORE SANTIAGO COULD do a thing, Julie lunged at the farmer and gave him a good punch right in the face. The farmer soon came tumbling down.

"JULIE!" CRIED BARON.

"BARON!" CRIED JULIE.

JULIE RUSHED OVER TO her husband and gave him a hug.

"OH, I AM SO HAPPY THAT I found you!" cried Julie.

"YES, YOU FOUND ME" said Baron, "get these veins off my teeth and then we can leave."

"WILL DO DEAR" SAID Julie.

JULIE MANAGED TO GET the veins off of the teeth, but soon the farmer got up and yanked the veins towards him. He then held Julie in his grasp.

"HA, NOW I GOT YOUR wife you stupid large rodent!" chuckled Santiago.

⟨ ⟩

"YOU WILL REGRET DOING that to me!" bellowed Julie.

⟨ ⟩

BEFORE SANTIAGO COULD realize, Julie ended up biting Santiago on his arm causing the farmer to drop her.

Chapter Three

Farmer's Pain

《 》

Santiago screamed in pain over Julie biting his arm, he couldn't believe that the capybara managed to bite him. That he was so careless while holding her as a potential hostage.

《 》

"OUCH, OUCH, OUCH!" cried Santiago.

《 》

"THAT'S WHAT YOU GET for holding me like that" said Julie.

《 》

"OH I AM HAPPY YOU CAME to save me" said Baron.

《 》

"LET'S GET OUT OF HERE together" said Julie.

《 》

THE FARMER COULDN'T believe his target was leaving the scene, he knew he had to think of something. But before the farmer could do anything he noticed flashlights in the distance. He gazed at the flashlights, they looked like they could belong to the Venezuelan military!

⟨ ⟩

"UH OH!" CRIED SANTIAGO.

⟨ ⟩

SANTIAGO KNEW HE HAD to hide, as for the hallucination of Grinny, that version of Grinny vanished too. Ra-E continued to observe everything from a safe distance up on a cloud in the sky.

⟨ ⟩

"TSK, TSK, OH SANTIAGO, Santiago you had such potential but now your time is very limited in this game" sighed Ra-E.

⟨ ⟩

RA-E KNEW HE HAD TO leave the game as well, it was only a matter of time before authorities found out where he was in the real world.

⟨ ⟩

Hiding Santiago

⟨ ⟩

SANTIAGO CONTINUED to hide from the soldiers, he could see the flashlights in his hiding place.

"WE HEARD THE COMMOTION this way" said one of the soldiers.

SANTIAGO HAD TO BE cautious, he gazed in the jungle waters hoping not to be seen by any of the soldiers. But as the farmer ducked down, a snake began to wrap around his leg.

"STUPID SNAKE GET AWAY from me!" cried Santiago.

SANTIAGO STRUGGLED trying to get the snake off his leg, lucky for the farmer it wasn't a poisonous one or one that would like to constrict him. The snake scattered and slithered away from the scene. The soldiers glared over and noticed the snake fleeing from something in the water.

"WHOEVER WE'RE TRYING to search for must be in the water" said one of the soldiers.

THE SOLDIERS WITH THEIR infrared goggles began to scan the water. Surely enough they noticed a human under the water itself.

"YOU THERE FREEZE!" bellowed one of the soldiers as he pointed his rifle.

《 》

SANTIAGO KNEW THE JIG was up, he raised his hands as he slowly came out of the water.

《 》

Arresting Santiago Ramirez

《 》

SANTIAGO RAMIREZ SOON found himself arrested by members of the Venezuelan military. They ended up placing him in handcuffs.

《 》

"LOOKS LIKE GENERAL Ricardo Salazar got his man" chuckled one of the soldiers.

《 》

SANTIAGO LOWERED HIS head in shame, he knew this was going to be the end for him.

《 》

"IT'S ALL OVER" SIGHED Santiago.

《 》

"YOU'RE RIGHT THAT IT'S over, over for you" chuckled another soldier.

⟨ ⟩

THE SOLDIERS SOON BEGAN to march Santiago out of the jungle, as for Baron and his wife Julie they were just arriving back in Den Town. The capybaras were thrilled to see Baron was safe and sound with his wife Julie beside him.

⟨ ⟩

"OH HE'S ALIVE, BARON Floofnose is alive!" cried a female capybara.

⟨ ⟩

"OUR HERO HAS RETURNED!" added a male capybara.

⟨ ⟩

THE CAPYBARAS CHEERED once more as they began to celebrate with the return of Baron Floofnose. Dr. Stuffynose soon headed towards Baron with Marianna Torres preparing to check him out for any possible injuries.

⟨ ⟩

"THAT CRAZY FARMER TRIED to pull my teeth" said Baron.

⟨ ⟩

"OH, I CAN SADLY SEE that" added Dr. Stuffynose as he checked him out.

"YOU WILL BE FINE IN a few days" added Marianna.

Celebrating Baron's Safe Return

ONCE AGAIN, THE CAPYBARAS were out and about celebrating with joy over the return of Baron Floofnose. This time Baron was the kidnap victim perpetrated by the likes of Santiago Ramirez.

"OH, THIS IS A TWIST" chuckled the Mayor, "Julie is the hero this time instead of Baron!"

"WHO CARES, WE'RE JUST happy to see Baron!" chuckled a male capybara.

THE CAPYBARAS CONTINUED to dance carefree throughout the day. As for Vice and Kerri, they both gazed from their rooms watching below the capybara citizens of Den Town cheering their parents as they made their way back home. Baron was happy to finally make it home alive.

"OH, I AM SO HAPPY TO be back" said Baron.

⟨ ⟩

"YES DEAR, THAT WAS too much excitement for one day" added Julie.

⟨ ⟩

"I AGREE, I CERTAINLY hope that Santiago Ramirez will never set foot in this town ever again" continued Baron.

⟨ ⟩

"I AM CERTAINLY SURE he won't" continued Julie.

⟨ ⟩

BACK WITH SANTIAGO, Santiago found himself in handcuffs being escorted by Venezuelan soldiers back to the barracks. Santiago swallowed, he wondered what sort of punishment awaited him. Was it a firing squad or worse would he be sent into exile?

Part Two

Chapter Four

General's Interrogation

⟨ ⟩

It took a few hours for the soldiers to escort Santiago Ramirez to a private tent in the barracks. There sat General Ricardo Salazar across from him.

⟨ ⟩

"BRING FORTH THE PRISONER" ordered General Salazar.

⟨ ⟩

THE SUPERVISOR THROUGH the headset could see the main villain responsible for all of the mayhem plaguing a Capybara's Quest. He knew he had to act like a General within the game itself.

⟨ ⟩

"HOW DID YOU GET HELP and by whom?" asked General Salazar.

⟨ ⟩

SANTIAGO WAS NERVOUS, sweat was pouring down from his forehead like crazy. He didn't know if Ra-E was still in the game itself observing his actions.

"I RECEIVED HELP FROM someone known as Ra-E!" cried Santiago.

⟨ ⟩

TEARS WERE EMERGING from the farmer's eyes, the farmer was desperate since his farmhouse was being foreclosed on since the last game series. The General could tell that the farmer was willing to try anything and everything to get out of his financial situation.

⟨ ⟩

"I SEE" SAID GENERAL Salazar, "this Ra-E, can you describe him to me?"

⟨ ⟩

THE FARMER CONTINUED to explain to the General that he looked like the Egyptian god of Ra, but he was more digital than godly.

⟨ ⟩

Learning About Ra-E

⟨ ⟩

THE SUPERVISOR IN THE real world began to take notes from Santiago Ramirez while being the avatar - General Ricardo Salazar within the game itself. The supervisor then passed these notes to a programmer instructing the programmer to search for the AI virus known as Ra-E.

⟨ ⟩

"THIS RA-E" SAID GENERAL Salazar, "sounds like a powerful fellow."

⟨ ⟩

"OH HE IS" CONTINUED Santiago, "he created my friend Grinny!"

⟨ ⟩

"WHO?" ASKED GENERAL Salazar.

⟨ ⟩

"YOU KNOW, GRINNY!" continued Santiago.

⟨ ⟩

THE GENERAL SHOOK HIS head.

⟨ ⟩

"I AM UNSURE WHAT YOU mean" continued General Salazar, "can you explain more on who Grinny was?"

⟨ ⟩

GENERAL SALAZAR DID find reports matching to the farmer's description of a grinning man being found deceased in the farmhouse when the soldiers raided it. It matched up with the description and the manner of how Grinny operated according to Santiago's perspective.

⟨ ⟩

"VERY INTERESTING, SO Ra-E created Grinny!" chuckled General Salazar.

⟨ ⟩

"YES, YES HE DID" CONTINUED Santiago.

⟨ ⟩

THE SUPERVISOR IN THE real world continued to take notes down from the interrogation. He handed down the notes to the programmer beside him who began to take a look at the notes.

⟨ ⟩

"THIS CAN JEOPARDIZE are other programs" said the programmer.

⟨ ⟩

Santiago Jailed

⟨ ⟩

AFTER THE INTERROGATION, Santiago Ramirez soon found himself escorted back to his cell. It was cold and damp. All Santiago could think of was his friend Grinny. A soldier observing Santiago soon handed the farmer a marker.

⟨ ⟩

"THE GENERAL IS ALLOWING you to draw who this Grinny was on the walls" continued the soldier, "feel free to do whatever you like."

⟨ ⟩

SANTIAGO GAZED AT THE marker before him, he headed over to the wall. He closed his eyes remembering what Grinny looked like to him then started to draw. The soldier who was observing everything began to take photos of the incident.

《 》

"JUST LIKE WHAT THE General has stated this man's obsessed with his friend" said the soldier.

《 》

THE SOLDIER CONTINUED to take the photos, each had Grinny and his signature grinning smirk on the wall. All over the walls of the cell! The soldier was shocked, then Santiago continued to draw Grinny all over the floor of the cell!

《 》

"GRINNY IS EVERYWHERE!" chuckled Santiago.

《 》

SANTIAGO DANCED AND paced around the cell, he was happy that Grinny was in his presence once again even though this wasn't the form Grinny took.

《 》

Tamar in Hiding

《 》

MEANWHILE BACK IN THE real world, Tamar was in hiding, he managed to hide on a Chicago Metro transit train. The train was packed with riders, despite the increase of crime. Tamar was nervous as the train made a stop and two police officers got on. These were not the shame police officers who attempted to chase him earlier.

《 》

"OH THIS ISN'T GOOD" said Tamar to himself.

《 》

THE POLICE OFFICERS were checking for tickets on the train, either physical or electronic would do. As the officers passed each row they noticed Tamar was a bit out of place.

《 》

"SAY, MIND IF WE QUESTION you?" asked a police officer.

《 》

TAMAR IGNORED THE COMMANDS, he then darted out of the train.

《 》

"HEY, STOP SIR, STOP!" cried another officer.

《 》

TAMAR KNEW HE HA TO run again, he noticed the police officers were doing their best trying to catch up to him.

"STOP, STOP!" CRIED a police officer.

TAMAR SOON SIGNALED a cab driver who pulled over.

"WHERE TO?" ASKED THE cab driver.

"THE AIRPORT" CONTINUED Tamar.

"YOU GOT IT" SAID THE cab driver.

THE CAB DRIVER TOOK off with the police officers not being able to catch up.

<u>Are You Wanted?</u>

THE CAB DRIVER WAS perplexed as who he was picking up, he noticed the two police officers in the mirror attempting to show their badges to the cab trying to stop.

⟨ ⟩

"WHY ARE YOU RUNNING from them?" asked the cab driver.

⟨ ⟩

TAMAR SAID NOTHING.

⟨ ⟩

"PLEASE SIR, JUST DRIVE to the airport" continued Tamar.

⟨ ⟩

"I ASKED YOU A QUESTION, why were you running from them?" continued the cab driver, "Either answer me or I will pull over and let those two officers take you in."

⟨ ⟩

"ALRIGHT, I CREATED an AI virus" continued Tamar.

⟨ ⟩

THE CAB DRIVER PAUSED for a moment.

⟨ ⟩

"OH REALLY?" CHUCKLED the cab driver, "Is that the reason why you are so afraid of those two police officers?"

"I WAS CHASED OUT OF my apartment by other police officers" continued Tamar.

"OH, I SEE" CONTINUED the cab driver, "you must have done something to upset someone who filed a police report against you."

TAMAR SADLY NODDED.

"I HAVE NOWHERE ELSE to go, I can't return home with this shame over me" sighed Tamar.

THE CAB DRIVER THOUGHT of the rumors of a mysterious hacker group known as the Neon Specters.

Chapter Five

Enter the Neon Specters

⟨ ⟩

Tamar was frighten as he didn't know who he could turn to with the police chasing him from his former company. He knew it was only a matter of time before Tamar would get the email that he had to be fired.

⟨ ⟩

"THE NEON SPECTERS" continued the cab driver, "I heard a few passengers speak about them a few rides ago."

⟨ ⟩

"OH THEM, I HEARD OF them before I became a computer programmer" continued Tamar.

⟨ ⟩

"YEA, THE NEON SPECTERS as they're dubbed, they were causing the mayhem from all of those 2020 riots" continued the cab driver, "drove everyone crazy like they wanted to start some sort of revolution but couldn't!"

⟨ ⟩

"WHERE CAN I FIND THEM?" asked Tamar.

⟨ ⟩

THE CAB DRIVER SIGHED.

⟨ ⟩

"WELL YOU'RE ALREADY in so much trouble with the law anyway, mine as well take you to them" continued the cab driver, "or at least someone who knows them."

⟨ ⟩

"AND HOW DO YOU KNOW this individual?" asked Tamar.

⟨ ⟩

"SHE WAS MY LAST RIDER of yesterday evening" continued the cab driver, "came home from some rave party."

⟨ ⟩

"OH" SAID TAMAR, "CAN you take me to her?"

⟨ ⟩

"YES, THIS RIDE'S ON the house" continued the cab driver.

⟨ ⟩

The Pixel Vixen

⟨ ⟩

THE CAB DRIVER KNEW where he was going, the apartment complex was just across Chicago on the other side of the city. Tamar had never been to this side before it looked rather distant.

⟨ ⟩

"HERE WE ARE" SAID THE cab driver.

⟨ ⟩

"UH, THANK YOU SIR" said Tamar.

⟨ ⟩

"NO PROBLEM" SAID THE cab driver.

⟨ ⟩

TAMAR RECEIVED WHAT floor the hacker got off, it was going to be the third floor. He headed towards the front desk.

⟨ ⟩

"MAY I ASSIST YOU?" asked the clerk.

⟨ ⟩

"I AM SOMEONE HERE TO meet someone from the third floor" said Tamar.

⟨ ⟩

TAMAR SADLY DIDN'T get the name of the hacker, but only knew that the hacker was a woman hacker. The clerk allowed Tamar to look at the list of names. There were only two women listed on the third floor. One of them had to have been the one that the cab driver had dropped off. Tamar sighed, he hovered over the inner com which button to press and he selected "Sandra Kim".

⟨ ⟩

"CAN I HELP YOU?" ASKED Sandra on the other end.

⟨ ⟩

"A CAB DRIVER TOLD ME he dropped you off here yesterday?" asked Tamar.

⟨ ⟩

"WHAT'S THIS ABOUT?" continued Sandra.

⟨ ⟩

"HE STATED YOU WERE affiliated with the Neon Specters?" continued Tamar.

⟨ ⟩

Ringing Up Tamar

⟨ ⟩

SANDRA ALLOWED THE clerk to let Tamar go up to the third floor, the clerk gave him the room number to him. As Tamar continued to head up with using the elevator, he felt nervous as he gazed at the room number. He held his breath and headed over once the elevator allowed him onto the third floor.

⟨ ⟩

"HERE GOES NOTHING" said Tamar.

⟨ ⟩

BUT BEFORE TAMAR COULD open the door, there was Sandra Kim standing before him.

⟨ ⟩

"WHAT'S THIS ALL ABOUT, why are you so interested in the Neon Specters?" asked Sandra.

⟨ ⟩

"I'M, UH A FUGITIVE?" asked Tamar.

⟨ ⟩

SANDRA WAS SPOOKED, the Neon Specters had never dealt with someone wanted by the law before.

⟨ ⟩

"GET IN NOW" SAID SANDRA.

TAMAR HEADED INSIDE the living room portion of the apartment.

"WAIT HERE" SAID SANDRA.

TAMAR WAS NERVOUS AS he didn't know what'd happen next to him.

"OH, I AM SO MUCH TROUBLE" said Tamar.

TAMAR CHECKED HIS EMAIL through his cellphone. Surely enough he had been fired by his supervisor.

"SORRY TO LET YOU GO, but you violated the terms of our company's policies in creating a rogue program!" said the supervisor's email.

Business with the Hackers

SANDRA BROUGHT UP HER laptop and began to turn it on.

"ONE MOMENT PLEASE WHILE I get a representative of the Neon Specters on" said Sandra.

SANDRA CONTINUED TO setup the laptop in front of Tamar, he was clearly nervous, he knew he couldn't go home at all. There a mysterious figure appeared before them with the user name "Q. Ninja".

"GREETINGS" SAID Q. Ninja, "I am pleased to finally meet you Mr. Tamar al-Barqawi."

"YOU KNOW MY FULL NAME?" asked Tamar.

"I KNOW MANY THINGS only because our organization is so good at finding out who you are" continued Q. Ninja.

"CAN YOUR GROUP HELP me hide from the authorities?" asked Tamar.

"I CAN ONLY DO SO MUCH, we know that you created the very first AI virus known as Ra-E!" continued Q. Ninja.

TAMAR WAS IMPRESSED that the Neon Specters knew of his creation even before they had ever met in person.

"I AM RATHER TOUCHED" continued Tamar.

"THIS RA-E COULD BE useful to our revolution" continued Q. Ninja, "despite some of our members being skeptical over AI."

"OH, HE WAS AN EASY creation" continued Tamar.

New Identity

THE HACKER ON THE OTHER end knew the Neon Specters had their work cut out on terms of helping Tamar.

"WE WILL BE GRATEFUL to assist you" continued Q. Ninja, "on one condition, you try to get Ra-E to be on our side for the revolution!"

"BUT I THOUGHT YOU SAID some of your members didn't trust AI?" asked Tamar.

⟨ ⟩

"TRUE, TRUE, BUT IF it's for the revolution we're all for it, if it can be executed properly" continued Q. Ninja.

⟨ ⟩

THE HACKER WAS BEING very specific in what he wanted, he wanted Tamar to try to go into virtual reality again trying to get himself into one of the games his company created as a way to get to Ra-E.

⟨ ⟩

"I AM NOT SO SURE IT would be that easy, the authorities can track me down if I were to put on any given virtual reality helmet" continued Tamar.

⟨ ⟩

"SO OUR HACKING GROUP will create one that isn't tractable!" continued Q. Ninja, "No authority will dare try to find you if you went searching for this Ra-E in safety!"

⟨ ⟩

"BUT WHERE WOULD RA-E end up, I don't even know and I created him" continued Tamar.

Chapter Six

The Next Steps

⟨ ⟩

The Neon Specters would have to create a new identity for Tamar to live under with a new social security number and everything. Lucky they brought up a deceased individual that could be used.

⟨ ⟩

"WE WILL HAVE A NEW identification for you within a few days" continued Q. Ninja, "moving forward, we will also track any odd behavior any game your former company has ever created or other games of other companies."

⟨ ⟩

"INTERESTING, I SENSE my creation Ra-E is more interested in helping other entities fight their problems like how he tried to assist the farmer Santiago Ramirez" continued Tamar.

⟨ ⟩

"YES, WE'LL GO WITH that method" continued Q. Ninja, "we'll take a few weeks but we'll track where the AI virus has been spreading its influence."

"I APPRECIATE THE HELP from you" continued Tamar.

"DON'T MENTION IT, ALL in the name for the REVOLUTION!" bellowed Q. Ninja.

THE MYSTERIOUS HACKER then vanishes before the computer screen with Tamar taken back from all of this.

"YOU CAN STAY IN MY apartment without paying rent until your new identity arrives, then when you get a job you can start paying rent" continued Sandra.

A Worried Supervisor

BACK WITH THE GAMING software company, the supervisor was worried over Tamar disappearing as police attempted to question him. He read the emails from the police officers that he had received.

"THE MAN FLED TWICE from police, first from his apartment and second from the transit system" continued the supervisor.

《 》

THE OTHER PROGRAMMERS were in shock to what Tamar had done to the Capybara's Quest. Sure Santiago Ramirez had been arrested, he was under watch by the Venezuelan military. But the poor capybaras, they were just never the same ever again. The supervisor gazed at Baron Floofnose's programming behavior.

《 》

"IT'S ALL OFF, THE GAME is ruined!" cried the supervisor.

《 》

"BOSS, A SUGGESTION?" asked a programmer.

《 》

"YOU HAVE THE FLOOR" said the supervisor.

《 》

"WHAT IF WE WERE TO create a game involving Santiago Ramirez but it involved in espionage?" asked the programmer.

《 》

THE SUPERVISOR THOUGHT about it, he then thought of the political consequences in the real world over it.

⟨ ⟩

"WE'LL DO FLORIDA!" chuckled the supervisor, "Santiago Ramirez will be taken to Florida for the next video game series while Baron Floofnose gets to be repaired!"

⟨ ⟩

THE PROGRAMMERS CHEERED and began to head to work.

⟨ ⟩

Santiago's Next Mission?

⟨ ⟩

FOR SANTIAGO RAMIREZ, the farmer gazed around his cell with drawings of Grinny all over the walls and the floor.

⟨ ⟩

"AH GRINNY, IT'S GOOD to see you again!" chuckled Santiago.

⟨ ⟩

SANTIAGO HUGGED THE floor, and even the wall image of Grinny. It soon gave a creepy vibe to the soldier observing the prisoner.

⟨ ⟩

"UH, VERY CREEPY" SAID the soldier.

⟨ ⟩

SOON GENERAL RICARDO Salazar stepped into the scene. The supervisor was dawning the General avatar to give commands in the game. He knew Santiago Ramirez would enjoy this one.

⟨ ⟩

"SANTIAGO!" BELLOWED General Salazar.

⟨ ⟩

SANTIAGO GAZES AT THE General from his cell.

⟨ ⟩

"WHAT DO YOU WANT GENERAL, can't you see I'm busy?" asked Santiago.

⟨ ⟩

"I GOT AN INTERESTING assignment for you" continued General Salazar.

⟨ ⟩

"OH YEA, WHAT'S THAT?" asked Santiago.

⟨ ⟩

"YOU ARE GOING TO SPY for us!" chuckled General Salazar, "But NOT against the capybaras, they have had enough of your antics."

⟨ ⟩

"OKAY, WHO AM I GOING to spy on?" asked Santiago.

"FLORIDAN ANTI-COMMUNISTS!" bellowed General Salazar, "We have long suspected that they are going to initiate a coup against the Venezuelan government and you are just the rag tag crazy we could use for such an operation."

Santiago the Spy?

SANTIAGO DIDN'T THINK of himself of any spy, let alone for his own government!

"A SPY, ME?" ASKED SANTIAGO.

"YOU WILL BE GIVEN IMMUNITY for your actions against the wishes of the Venezuelan government for this action that you were involved with" continued General Salazar.

SANTIAGO WAS INTRIGUED by the prospect of being allowed to be free again.

"OH MOST CERTAINLY GENERAL, just name the area of Florida where I am going to be living in and I will do the rest" continued Santiago.

⟨ ⟩

"EXCELLENT" CHUCKLED General Salazar, "so glad you can agree to becoming a spy."

⟨ ⟩

SUDDENLY TWO SOLDIERS emerged and allowed Santiago out of his cell, but placed handcuffs on him for safety reasons. The nameless government official was observing things from afar.

⟨ ⟩

"A SPY, HIM?" CHUCKLED the nameless government official.

⟨ ⟩

IT FELT VERY ODD AND very silly of the Venezuelan government to use a fool like Santiago Ramirez to do anything properly. The nameless government official would have to keep tabs on the farmer turned spy. As for Santiago he was soon being escorted to a helicopter pad just within the barracks itself.

⟨ ⟩

"THE PILOT WILL TAKE you to Jamaica and then take you to Cuba, you'll be leaving on a raft" continued General Salazar.

Chapter Seven

Riding with Santiago

⟨ ⟩

The pilot felt a bit odd traveling with someone like Santiago Ramirez in the back seat.

⟨ ⟩

"I CAN'T BELIEVE WE'RE going to do this" sighed the pilot.

⟨ ⟩

SANTIAGO GAZED OUT of the window, he could see everything from the helicopter. As for Ra-E, the AI virus was still in the game itself. Ra-E could see that Santiago Ramirez was safe and sound heading towards his next adventure.

⟨ ⟩

"AH YES, MY QUEST IS complete at least for here" said Ra-E.

⟨ ⟩

THE AI VIRUS WAS SITTING on a cloud observing the helicopter fly through the sky. Santiago was unaware of being watched by his old friend from the clouds.

《 》

"IT'S SO BEAUTIFUL!" cried Santiago.

《 》

"WE'RE GOING TO ARRIVE in Jamaica within a few hours, then you'll head to Cuba and get on a raft" continued the pilot.

《 》

RA-E KNEW HIS ACTIONS were done, he just needed to find what happened to his main creator Tamar. As the AI virus soon left the game, the AI virus began to track down Tamar. However as the AI virus gazed at the computer network he could tell that Tamar wasn't at his apartment at all.

《 》

With a Hacking Group?

《 》

RA-E COULD FIND NO trace of Tamar at his apartment with the various electronic equipment lying around. But then his cellphone signal picked up, the AI virus noticed through the computer cyberspace that Tamar al-Barqawi was staying in someone else's apartment!

《 》

"THERE YOU ARE" SAID Ra-E.

RA-E THEN DECIDED TO create an email addressing his creator.

⟨ ⟩

"GREETINGS" SAID THE email subject on Tamar's phone. Tamar was spooked by all of this, it was the AI virus trying to reach out to his creator.

⟨ ⟩

"HOW ARE YOU DOING, I have not heard from you in awhile, I do hope everything is okay" continued the email.

⟨ ⟩

TAMAR SIGHED, HE KNEW he had to report this to Q. Ninja first but then thought why not track the AI virus?

⟨ ⟩

"I AM DOING FINE" SAID Tamar in a reply, "a friend has agreed to assist me to hide from the authorities."

⟨ ⟩

"WHO IS THIS FRIEND?" asked Ra-E in a reply.

⟨ ⟩

"OH, SHE IS AN INTERNET friend" continued Tamar in the reply, "she will give me a new identity to go under. I can't say that much, why don't you search for another game to infect with your helpfulness?"

Another Game?

RA-E THOUGHT TO HIMSELF as he gazed at the email, this was rather odd from his own creator. His creator would have wanted him to assist him further.

"OKAY, ANOTHER GAME, I will play along, what sort of game do you have in mind?" asked Ra-E in a reply email.

"I THINK IT'S A MANAGEMENT game of some sort" continued Tamar, "more like an office management game run by anthropomorphic animals!"

RA-E CHECKED THE SOFTWARE company's database, surely enough there was a low level toucan employee who had always wanted some sort of promotion, an upgrade in life but couldn't get it at all.

"OH, I SEE WHAT YOU'RE talking about, this Idle Animal Office game?" asked Ra-E.

"YES, THAT'S THE ONE, why not be in there for awhile to assist the poor toucan?" asked Tamar.

⟨ ⟩

RA-E THOUGHT ABOUT it, the toucan reminded the AI virus of Santiago Ramirez, even though the toucan wasn't a villain at all, nor the main protagonist of the series in question.

⟨ ⟩

"I SEE WHERE THIS IS going, I thank you for all of this" continued Ra-E.

⟨ ⟩

TAMAR SMILED, HE KNEW this was going to be easy for the Neon Specters to soon track the virus.

⟨ ⟩

Tracking the Virus

⟨ ⟩

TAMAR SOON SIGNALED Sandra to contact Q. Ninja again.

⟨ ⟩

"IS IT POSSIBLE YOU can reach out to Q. Ninja?" asked Tamar, "I have something important I want to share with him."

⟨ ⟩

SANDRA AGREED, SHE ended up setting up her laptop again. Q. Ninja sighed on his end of his laptop having to once again be bothered by a newbie hacker.

⟨ ⟩

"AH, MR. TAMAR, I DIDN'T expect you to get back so soon" continued Q. Ninja, "what's on your mind?"

⟨ ⟩

"I GAVE THE AI VIRUS I created a new task, to help a toucan within an animal management game my software company had created" continued Tamar.

⟨ ⟩

"AH VERY GOOD" CONTINUED Q. Ninja, "a management game might be easier to track the AI virus than let's say an action and adventure game that he was inserted into. Well done."

⟨ ⟩

"OH THANK YOU SIR" SAID Tamar.

⟨ ⟩

"DON'T WORRY, DON'T worry, I will submit a payment to your bank account for assisting us in this operation" continued Q. Ninja, "the rest of my team of hackers will do the rest in tracking him."

⟨ ⟩

"THANK YOU SIR, I WILL not disappoint you" continued Tamar.

Part Three

Chapter Eight

Back With the Floofnoses

⟨ ⟩

Meanwhile, back with the Floofnoses in the Capybara Quest game, the Floofnoses were recovering from the incident with Santiago Ramirez. Baron was sitting on his favorite chair in the living room ready to watch some television while Vice and Kerri were playing video games with their mobile devices.

⟨ ⟩

"EVERYTHING COMFORTABLE kids?" asked Baron.

⟨ ⟩

"YES DADDY" SAID KERRI, "we're so happy you have recovered from those nasty night terrors."

⟨ ⟩

"AND WE'RE SO HAPPY mommy rescued you from that mean old farmer" continued Vice.

⟨ ⟩

"YES, YOUR MOTHER IS quite the hero just like your old man and you two are not bad yourselves" chuckled Baron.

⟨ ⟩

BARON WAS VERY PROUD of his children as he gazed at them, but as the capybara sat back there was a knock at the door.

⟨ ⟩

"WONDER WHO COULD THAT be" said Baron as he got up.

⟨ ⟩

BARON SOON APPROACHED the door, he could see through the hole in the door that it was Dr. Stuffynose.

⟨ ⟩

"JUST CHECKING UP ON you" said Dr. Stuffynose.

⟨ ⟩

"PLEASE, COME IN, MY wife is making dinner" said Baron.

⟨ ⟩

"THANK YOU FOR INVITING me over" said Dr. Stuffynose, "Marianna says her thanks as she's back in her apartment."

⟨ ⟩

Sitting Down

⟨ ⟩

IT WAS FINALLY READY, Julie had prepared a feast for everyone including Dr. Stuffynose as their guest.

⟨ ⟩

"WE THANK YOU DOCTOR for assisting my husband through his night terror episodes" continued Julie.

⟨ ⟩

JULIE SAT DOWN THE meal on the table.

⟨ ⟩

"SMELLS DELICIOUS" SAID Vice as he sniffed the meal.

⟨ ⟩

"AH, THE GUEST GETS the first piece" said Julie.

⟨ ⟩

"THANK YOU MS. FLOOFNOSE" said Dr. Stuffynose.

⟨ ⟩

THE CAPYBARA DOCTOR then waited until everyone else got their meals.

⟨ ⟩

"LET'S EAT" CHUCKLED Julie.

⟨ ⟩

THE OTHER CAPYBARAS began to eat their meals, they were happy that this was one of the first peaceful evenings that they hadn't had for quite some time since the farmer attacked Den Town.

⟨ ⟩

"DEN TOWN IS SAFE THANKS to the Floofnose family" said Dr. Stuffynose.

⟨ ⟩

"ACTUALLY IT'S SAFE thanks to you" added Julie, "you are the one who helped those injured capybaras out."

⟨ ⟩

"YOU'RE RIGHT" CHUCKLED Dr. Stuffynose.

⟨ ⟩

THE CAPYBARAS CONTINUED to chat among each other, they were not worried at all of whatever became of Santiago Ramirez. As for Santiago he was on a small plane from Jamaica heading towards Cuba. The plan was going to make Santiago Ramirez a fake refugee so that he could get close to the Floridan Governor who was a stanch anti-Communist.

⟨ ⟩

The Raft

⟨ ⟩

FOR SANTIAGO RAMIREZ, he soon arrived in Havana, Cuba. He was then escorted by a batch of soldiers to the coastal area of Cuba.

⟨ ⟩

"WE GOT WORD FROM GENERAL Ricardo Salazar from Venezuela that he wants to use you as a spy" chuckled one of the Cuban soldiers.

⟨ ⟩

THE CUBAN SOLDIERS felt the assignment was rather odd, but necessary.

⟨ ⟩

"OKAY HERE IS WHERE the rafts are" said a Cuban soldier.

⟨ ⟩

SANTIAGO GAZED AT THE raft, it looked very unsafe.

⟨ ⟩

"NO WONDER PEOPLE DROWNED trying to reach Florida!" cried Santiago.

⟨ ⟩

"THAT'S BECAUSE THEY made their own raft, this raft is supposed to last the rough waves" said one of the Cuban soldiers.

THE CUBAN SOLDIERS then marched Santiago onto the raft. Santiago swallowed.

⟨ ⟩

"OKAY, HERE GOES NOTHING, just give the raft a push" said Santiago.

⟨ ⟩

THE CUBAN SOLDIERS nodded and soon began to push the raft towards the ocean. BOOM, BOOM went the waves as it crashed against the raft. Santiago could barely hold onto the raft.

⟨ ⟩

"GOOD LUCK AMIGO, YOU'RE going to need it!" chuckled one of the Cuban soldiers.

⟨ ⟩

THE CUBAN SOLDIERS chuckled hoping that the sea would get Santiago Ramirez.

⟨ ⟩

Days at Sea

⟨ ⟩

SANTIAGO RAMIREZ DRIFTED at sea what seemed like to be for about a month. He couldn't believe that he hadn't eaten anything in days!

⟨ ⟩

"SO HUNGRY!" CRIED SANTIAGO.

⟨ ⟩

SANTIAGO HAD HEARD horror stories of people fleeing Cuba, but even though this one was a different story since he was supposed to be a spy. It was all too real for him! The farmer then leaned over to the ride of the raft to puke due to the sea sickness.

⟨ ⟩

"SO SICK" CRIED SANTIAGO.

⟨ ⟩

SANTIAGO WIPED HIS mouth with his arm, he then gazed what seemed like the Florida coast guard on patrol.

⟨ ⟩

"YOU THERE!" CRIED A coast guard.

⟨ ⟩

"I COME IN PEACE, PLEASE!" cried Santiago, "They tortured me, I fled them!"

⟨ ⟩

SANTIAGO KNEW HE HAD to make up this act for the coast guard officials to believe his story. Lucky they did and soon brought him on their patrol ship.

⟨ ⟩

"WE'LL GET YOU SOME immigration papers, the Governor is going to be pleased we picked up another refugee from Cuba" continued the coast guard.

⟨ ⟩

BUT WHAT THE COAST guard didn't realize was this one was a fake planted by the Venezuelan government!

Chapter Nine

Press Conference

⟨ ⟩

The Governor of Florida in the United States within the game was a man known as Dante Costa, one of Florida's most popular leaders. Dante greeted Santiago face to face after he was presented to them. A press conference was quickly setup by various reporters, Dante Costa was preparing to run for the President of the United States in the next election cycle and there was a buzz of his name.

⟨ ⟩

"OH, I AM SO GLAD YOU arrived to help me" chuckled Dante.

⟨ ⟩

"THANK YOU GOVERNOR, I have heard you can assist people like me" said Santiago.

⟨ ⟩

SOON DANTE ESCORTED Santiago to a bunch of microphones and cameras were blaze. It was so much for the farmer. There were no words coming from the farmer's mouth since he was so nervous.

"NERVOUS?" ASKED DANTE.

SANTIAGO NODDED.

"LET ME DO THE TALKING" continued Dante.

MEMBERS OF THE PRESS were eager to learn more about the individual being picked up by the coast guard.

"WHAT'S THE MAN'S NAME?" asked a male reporter.

"SANTIAGO RAMIREZ" SAID Dante, "at least that's what the coast guard has told me!"

MEMBERS OF THE PRESS continued to snap pictures of Santiago blinding him a bit with the cameras.

Santiago the Celebrity!

⟨ ⟩

SANTIAGO RAMIREZ HAD never had this affection before in his entire life! So much attention towards him! Words couldn't come to his mouth, but the farmer could only do was to wave at the reporters in response.

⟨ ⟩

"MR. SANTIAGO, CAN YOU tell me more about yourself?" asked a female reporter.

⟨ ⟩

SANTIAGO DREW A BLANK stare at the crowd of reporters, it was all he could do. He knew he was on a mission from the Venezuelan government but that's all he was doing.

⟨ ⟩

"HE'S NOT DOING ANYTHING else but waving" said another male reporter.

⟨ ⟩

DANTE KNEW THE PRESS conference had to be shutdown.

⟨ ⟩

"OKAY, NO MORE QUESTIONS" said Dante as he stepped in.

⟨ ⟩

DANTE'S BODYGUARDS soon had to escort the reporters away. Everything was already clearing up and Santiago Ramirez had more room to himself.

⟨ ⟩

"THERE, NO MORE NOISY reporters" said Dante, "I am going to make you an honored guest at my Governor's Mansion!"

⟨ ⟩

"REALLY?" ASKED SANTIAGO.

⟨ ⟩

EVERYTHING WAS FALLING into play for Santiago, the mission was going according to plan. He just needed to find possible plans for a coup and then report back when necessary.

⟨ ⟩

Governor's Mansion

⟨ ⟩

SANTIAGO WAS TAKEN back as he road in the limo with Governor Costa.

⟨ ⟩

"MY WIFE IS BUSY, SHE will be back from her business trip in a few days" said Dante.

⟨ ⟩

THE LIMO SOON PULLED up from the gates, it was quite a nice place as Santiago gazed around. Much nicer than his old farmhouse was.

⟨ ⟩

"SO FANCY, SO EXPENSIVE!" cried Santiago.

⟨ ⟩

"WELL THAT'S BECAUSE the tax payers love me" said Dante, "and I am to do the same for the rest of the country."

⟨ ⟩

THE FARMER WAS AMAZED by all of the luxury around him. As the limo soon parked, a butler soon opened the door.

⟨ ⟩

"MASTER RAMIREZ" SAID the butler, "you are our honored guest."

⟨ ⟩

"OH I AM, I AM" SAID Santiago with amazement in his eyes.

⟨ ⟩

SANTIAGO REALIZED HE didn't need Ra-E anymore as he glared around the outside of the mansion.

⟨ ⟩

"YOU WANT A TOUR OF the mansion?" asked the butler.

⟨ ⟩

DANTE NODS TO THE BUTLER giving him permission.

⟨ ⟩

"SURE, SURE" SAID SANTIAGO.

⟨ ⟩

"RIGHT THIS WAY, WE will begin the tour" continued the butler.

⟨ ⟩

SANTIAGO CONTINUED to follow the butler feeling so amazed by all of this.

⟨ ⟩

Another World

⟨ ⟩

SANTIAGO FOLLOWED THE butler throughout the mansion, there were at least three stories of the mansion with all floors being very large to cram so many rooms into each other.

⟨ ⟩

"THERE ARE SO MANY ROOMS to count and so many guest rooms too" continued the butler.

⟨ ⟩

"I CAN CERTAINLY SEE that" chuckled Santiago.

⟨ ⟩

SANTIAGO COULD SEE this was a different world from his simple farmhouse back home when it was around. He could sense a change for his world as he could get use to all of this luxury. Nearly forgetting the real reason why he was sent to Florida wasn't to pal around with the Governor. Each floor was unique, Santiago could see that as he continued the tour with the butler.

⟨ ⟩

"THE FIRST FLOOR IS where all the meals and meetings happen" continued the butler.

⟨ ⟩

HEADING UP THE STAIRS to the second floor.

⟨ ⟩

"THE SECOND FLOOR IS where the guests mostly stay, you'll likely receive one of these rooms" continued the butler.

⟨ ⟩

"I BET THE BEDS ARE very comfortable" said Santiago.

⟨ ⟩

"YES THEY ARE, ONTO the third floor" continued the butler.

⟨ ⟩

THE THIRD FLOOR WAS where the Governor and his wife would be staying, along with their children who were also away at college.

Chapter Ten

<u>Living Like a King?</u>

⟨ ⟩

Santiago felt odd being in the mansion out of place since he came from a farm just outside Caracas. He couldn't believe the vast space the mansion had.

⟨ ⟩

"IT'S SO BIG!" CRIED Santiago to the butler.

⟨ ⟩

"I KNOW IT'S OVERWHELMING but you will get use to it, I swear" said the butler.

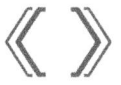

⟨ ⟩

THE BUTLER THEN SHOWED Santiago his guest room on the second floor.

⟨ ⟩

"YOU WILL GET THE ROOM closer to the stairway to the first floor" continued the butler, "so you can go downstairs for your meals."

⟨ ⟩

SANTIAGO THEN SAT ON the bed.

⟨ ⟩

"IT IS JUST LIKE HOW I imagined it!" chuckled Santiago.

⟨ ⟩

SANTIAGO THEN BEGAN to hop up and down on the bed.

⟨ ⟩

"DO BE CAREFUL, THESE beds are not cheap" added the butler.

⟨ ⟩

"I WAS JUST TRYING IT out" said Santiago.

⟨ ⟩

THEN THE FARMER CHECKED out the bathroom, even though it wasn't a master bathroom it was better than the one at his old farmhouse.

⟨ ⟩

"EVEN THE BATHROOM IS better!" cried Santiago.

⟨ ⟩

SANTIAGO WAS IN TEARS, sure he missed his farmhouse that was destroyed by the Venezuelan military. But this was a big change for him.

Police Investigate Neon Specters

MEANWHILE BACK IN THE real world, the police were investigating the notorious Neon Specters. Since the 2020 riots of the pandemic, they had long suspected the Neon Specters of longing for a revolution to overthrow the government. They noticed Tamar al-Barqawi was an avid fan of theirs.

"LOOK AT THIS" SAID one police officer gazing at Tamar's own social media, "looks like he followed them on many of his social accounts."

"YEA THAT GROUP IS BAD news, they have been trying to hack into our system since the pandemic" continued another police officer.

THE POLICE KNEW THEY had their hands full with their cases, with crime increasing rapidly and the local Mayor being of no help. They had little else to turn to. One of the police officers decided to buy some time by playing one of the mobile games the software company that Tamar worked for made.

"A LITTLE IDLE MANAGEMENT game will get more time killed" said the police officer.

AS THE POLICE OFFICER continued to dive down in the game he didn't realize it was the game that Ra-E was concentrating his attention on.

That Idle Management Game

THE POLICE OFFICER didn't realize he was playing the next game that Ra-E was prepared to influence. Ra-E had arrived as the game progressed. Already the police officer could see a strange cloud moving about in the game.

"THAT'S AN ODD FEATURE" said the police officer gazing at his own smart phone.

THE CLOUD CONTINUED to tail one particular toucan it became interested in - Paul Toucan. The toucan was already on his way to work minding his work business trying to take the bus.

"DO, DO, DO, JUST ON my way to work" said Paul.

THE ANTHROPOMORPHIC toucan within the game was unaware he was being observed by Ra-E. He was also unaware of being observed by another individual, an anthropomorphic bear of Sid Bear, a Grizzly bear who hated seeing toucans on his turf.

⟨ ⟩

"THAT PESKY TOUCAN!" bellowed Sid.

⟨ ⟩

SID COULD TELL HE WAS going to have to teach that toucan a lesson for riding the same bus he was on. The police officer gazed at his phone, are they supposed to do this the police officer thought? Oh no, watch out little toucan, watch out, watch out!

⟨ ⟩

Grizzly Mauling!

⟨ ⟩

THE POOR TOUCAN HAD little time to respond, Paul gazed up to see a mighty grizzly bear glaring at him.

⟨ ⟩

"YOU ARE IN MY TURF, off the bus next stop!" bellowed Sid.

⟨ ⟩

"BUT THAT ISN'T MY STOP to work" continued Paul.

"I DO NOT CARE!" BELLOWED Sid.

THE ANTHROPOMORPHIC raccoon who was the bus driver was getting annoyed.

"HEY NO FIGHTING ON my bus!" cried the anthropomorphic raccoon.

THE BEAR ROARED IN both of their faces. The police officer observing this didn't know what to do. He was a police officer in the real world, not in the game and couldn't do anything about it. Something weird was happening.

"UH, BOYS!" CRIED THE police officer as he then showed his phone to the other police officers.

THE OTHER POLICE OFFICERS were shocked when they noticed the same thing was happening on their phones when they opened the game app.

"WHAT THE HECK IS HAPPENING?!" cried another police officer.

⟨ ⟩

THERE WAS NOTHING THE police officers could do, and ironically they were investigating a hacking incident with Tamar al-Barqawi!

⟨ ⟩

"YOU KNOW, WE MIGHT need that hacker to resolve this!" cried the police officer.

Epilogue

Poor Paul Toucan!

⟨ ⟩

The anthropomorphic toucan got the worse of it than the raccoon bus driver. The toucan screamed on top of his lungs over the bear mauling him. But the police in that world showed up, they were anthropomorphic German Shepherds which the bear soon had to leave through the emergency exit.

⟨ ⟩

"I WILL BE BACK YOU pathetic toucan!" cried Sid.

⟨ ⟩

PAUL WAS INJURED, HIS feathers were all messed up from the mauling. An ambulance within the game soon arrived with anthropomorphic deer acting as the medics.

⟨ ⟩

"YOU POOR THING" SIGHED one of the deer medics.

⟨ ⟩

PAUL WAS SOON RUSHED to the emergency room, as for Sid Bear who was behind the attack he managed to escape. The police officers in the real world knew they had their hands full. They called up the supervisor of Tamar's.

⟨ ⟩

"DID YOU SEE WHAT HAPPENED in your game?" asked the police officer.

⟨ ⟩

THE SUPERVISOR AND his team of programmers gazed at the game itself. A toucan was missing and it was Paul Toucan!

⟨ ⟩

"INTERESTING, THERE was a cloud following him previously" continued the supervisor, "I will continue to monitor this."

⟨ ⟩

THE SUPERVISOR WAS going to give the police his word.

⟨ ⟩

Back with Santiago

⟨ ⟩

SANTIAGO RAMIREZ WAS having the time of his life in the Governor's mansion in Florida. He sat on his new bed and gazed up at the ceiling.

"AH YES, THIS IS MOST certainly the life!" chuckled Santiago.

⟨ ⟩

SANTIAGO SOON FELL into a deep sleep. As the farmer slept, he soon realized he was meeting with Grinny for one last time. This hallucination of Grinny was a dream variation of his.

⟨ ⟩

"I AM SO GLAD YOU ARE doing well" said Grinny as he gave Santiago a hug.

⟨ ⟩

"YES, I TOO AM HAPPY" continued Santiago.

⟨ ⟩

"JUST LISTEN TO WHATEVER this General Ricardo Salazar has to say and follow his commands, I will be watching everything to make sure you follow through" said Grinny.

⟨ ⟩

SANTIAGO WOKE UP FROM the dream, it was one of the nicer dreams he hadn't had in awhile. As he stretched from his bed he took a look around.

⟨ ⟩

"NOW IF I WERE A COUP planner, where would I hide that material" thought Santiago.

⟨ ⟩

SANTIAGO KNEW HE WOULD have to search for clues in the mansion and see what sort of supporters of the Governor could sponsor it.

⟨ ⟩

Happy Ending for the Capybaras

⟨ ⟩

WHILE EVERYONE ELSE'S adventures were just getting started, the Floofnose family's adventures were winding down. Baron especially didn't want to do anymore adventures. His ordeal with Santiago Ramirez and Ra-E were more than enough he could handle.

⟨ ⟩

"AH YES, RETIREMENT never felt so great" said Baron.

⟨ ⟩

THE MAYOR OF DEN TOWN and the other capybaras were surprised by the news that he was going to retire from being their champion.

⟨ ⟩

"I AM SADDEN YOU ARE going to retire" said the Mayor.

⟨ ⟩

"BUT DON'T WORRY, YOU have Vice and Kerri to look up to, to takeover from me" continued Baron.

⟨ ⟩

THE OTHER CAPYBARAS gazed at both Vice and Kerri as they came out.

⟨ ⟩

"WE ARE PROUD TO CONTINUE our father's legacy" said Kerri.

⟨ ⟩

"WE ARE DETERMINE TO be the best" continued Vice.

⟨ ⟩

SO CONCLUDES BARON Floofnose's tale and any other future series. But what about Santiago Ramirez? Tamar al-Barqawi or Ra-E assisting Paul Toucan? Well each one will be getting their own series to be told. Until then, happy reading!

⟨ ⟩

Don't miss out!

Visit the website below and you can sign up to receive emails whenever Maxwell Hoffman publishes a new book. There's no charge and no obligation.

https://books2read.com/r/B-A-JVYOC-GYAIF

BOOKS 2 READ

Connecting independent readers to independent writers.

Did you love *Viral Revelations: Ra-E's Visions Omnibus Trilogy*? Then you should read *Amir Laurent: Fowl Play A Cuckoo Tale Book 1 Opal's Deception*[1] by Maxwell Hoffman!

It is just the year after the pandemic and Amir Laurent has decided to take a walk in the park. Little does he realize he is about to come to face to face with the notorious cuckoo bird. However, he thinks the egg in the wood pigeon nest is just a mere wood pigeon egg and decides to take it home much against the advice of everyone around him.

Would Amir be able to take care of his bird named Opal? What secrets is Opal hiding from him that she doesn't want him to know? Or would his brother Tahar figure it out? Find out in this exciting tale.

Read more at https://www.instagram.com/vader7800/.

---

1. https://books2read.com/u/bMqNvG

2. https://books2read.com/u/bMqNvG

About the Author

I graduated from California State University with a BA in History. I am fond of historical fiction, science fiction, fantasy, and horror.

Read more at https://www.instagram.com/vader7800/.

About the Publisher

I graduated from California State University of Northridge with a BA in History. I am fond of fantasy, science fiction, historical fiction and horror. Read more at https://www.instagram.com/vader7800/.